Gallium Girl

a novel of supernaturals

Tyree Campbell

Gallium Girl
by Tyree Campbell

All rights reserved. No part of this book may be reproduced or transmitted in any form or by any means, electronic or mechanical, including photocopying or recording or by any information storage and retrieval systems, without expressed written consent of the author and/or artists.

Gallium Girl is a work of fiction. Names, characters, places, and incidents are products of the author's imagination. Any resemblance to actual events or persons, living or dead, is entirely coincidental.

Story copyright owned by Tyree Campbell
Cover illustration "The Pod" and cover design by Marcia A. Borell

First Printing, June 2024

Hiraeth Publishing
P.O. Box 1248
Tularosa, NM 88352
e-mail: hiraethsubs@yahoo.com

Visit www.hiraethsffh.com for online science fiction, fantasy, horror, scifaiku, and more. Stop by our online bookstore for novels, magazines, anthologies, and collections. **Support the small, independent press...and your First Amendment rights.**

Also by Tyree Campbell

Nyx Series (Novels):
Nyx: Malache
Nyx: Mystere
Nyx: The Protectors
Nyx: Pangaea
Nyx: The Redoubt

Yoelin Thibbony Rescues (Novels)
The Butterfly and the Sea Dragon *
The Moth and the Flame *
*The Thursday Child**
Avatar
The End of Innocence

Lark Series (Novels)
The Desert Lark
The Iphajean Lark
The Justice Lark
The Traffic Lark
The Illusion Lark

Novels:
*The Adventures of Colo Collins &
Tama Toledo in Space and Time*
*The Adventures of Colo Collins &
Tama Toledo in Love and in Trouble*
Aoife's Kiss
The Breathless Stars
The Dice of God
The Dog at the Foot of the Bed
The Dog at War
Gallium Girl
Heir Apparent
Indigo

Iuliae: Past Tense
The Quinx Effect
Starwinders: Nohana's Heart
Starwinders: Nohana's Triangles
Thuvia, Maid of Earth
A Wolf to Guard the Door
The Woman from the Institute

Superheroine Novellas:
Bombay Sapphire 1 **
Bombay Sapphire 2 **
Bombay Sapphire 3 **
Bombay Sapphire 4 **
Bombay Sapphire 5
Oliva Sudden 1
Peridot 1
Peridot 2
Peridot 3
Peridot 4
Voyeuse 1
Voyeuse 2
Voyeuse 3

Collections:
AbracaDrabble
Drink Before the War
A Nice Girl Like You
(published by Khimairal, Inc)
Quantum Women *

Novellas:
Becoming Jade
Cloudburst
Future Tense
The Girl on the Dump
The Martian Women
Sabit the Sumerian
Sarrow

Poetry Collections
A Danger to Self and Others

SF for Younger Readers
Pyra and the Tektites 1
Pyra (graphic novel) 1
Pyra and the Tektites 2
Pyra (graphic novel) 2
Pyra and the Tektites 3
Pyra and the Tektites 4
Pyra and the Tektites 5
Pyra and the Tektites 6

* published by Nomadic Delirium Press

** published by Pro Se Press

All titles are available from the Shop at www.hiraethsffh.com

For David Blalock

001: The New World

The dreadful sounds coming from the area of the cooler in the rear of the store invested Mollie with more than the usual apprehensions about her job: a woman, alone, late night, convenience store. She always labored with those four strikes against her—five, counting her real name—and she'd hardly been up to bat. But the sounds were something else entirely.

Mollie had only just become aware of them, because they had been so strange that she'd had no point of reference for them, and therefore they could not be. But the snuffling and smacking were insistent, and she realized that they had been going on for some time. Minutes, perhaps. Standing on the slightly elevated floor behind the register, she listened with growing trepidation. She sought to place the noises in a familiar context, something in her experience. An image coalesced in her mind, of a frustrated plumber using a plunger to unclog a toilet that had been stuffed with marshmallows. The image explained the growling and the *thucks* and the *snarfs*. But there was no plumber in the store. There was, in fact, as far as she knew, no one else in the store.

Maybe someone came in while I was stocking the chips. Yes, that could be. It's just a late-night customer, grousing.

Only this, she recalled, from Poe, *and nothing more.*

He could not have entered through the back door. She had locked it just after seven, three hours ago. *Didn't I lock it? Oh, God . . .*

As the uncertainty shredded her nerves, she glanced up at the security mirrors. The aisles were empty. The mirror that reflected the back of the store was still out of alignment—Carson had promised to have it reset, but the store manager did not have to work the late shift, hence the procrastination—but Mollie caught a glimpse of a reflection in the glass doors of the cooler. Something dark hunched near the sour cream. *What the hell . . . ?*

Her heart felt like a cooked turkey giblet, lodged in her throat. It gave her contralto a tremulous note. "Everything OK back there?" she called.

The darkness seemed to shift. It's not a shadow, she thought. The notion entered her mind then that Bigfoot had migrated to southeastern Arizona and was now scavenging for party dip. This was impossible, of course, but there was a costume rental here in Sierra Vista, and perhaps he was on the way to a party somewhere. Mollie herself had once toyed with the idea of attending a Halloween party dressed as Mary Marvel, the superhero wife of Captain Marvel. If she stopped slouching, her figure could handle the red tights, but her hair was straw-yellow and long and straight, not golden and curly, not suitably superheroish, and her eyes were not cornflower blue but a sort of not-quite-jade-not-quite-serpentine. Instead, not a party person, she had opted for a nightshirt and bed. Now she wished Bigfoot would follow her lead.

Something solid yet soft thudded to the floor, like a glob of dough. The frozen biscuits were in that area. Had he opened a tube of them? If so, why? As she stepped down from behind the register a tiny internal voice told her to call the police, but the mystery had already hooked her, like a scab that just had to be worried loose to see if the wound had healed. Most times, a little dot of blood formed, because the scab had been removed too soon. But that never stopped you from worrying the next one loose.

"Hello?"

The sounds stopped momentarily, then resumed with vigor. "Insignificance becomes me," Mollie muttered. She crept closer to the end of the aisle, but as she prepared to turn left, to confront the customer, something flew past her into the canned soups next to her and tumbled to the floor. Mollie stifled a yelp, and looked down at the remains of an oblong, waxed cardpaper carton. The end had been shredded, and marked by what appeared to be tooth prints, as if the customer had been desperate to get at the goodies inside. To get at Luanne's Extra Firm Tofu.

Mollie stood up, rounded the end of the aisle, and yelled, "What's going on here?" quite before she recognized what she was confronting. A dark shape rose up on hind legs, freezing her in her tracks. A *werewolf?* No . . . a man in a werewolf costume. The muzzle of his mask was smeared with tofu. It dripped from his fangs and his paws, and tiny globs of it festooned his chest fur.

Knowing a confrontation was imminent, Mollie felt her heart race. She was on the verge of pointing out to the festive customer that he was going to have to pay for all the tofu he had consumed on the premises when he lowered his head slightly, and looked directly into her eyes.

Wrong again, she realized. It *is* a werewolf.

It charged her. Petrified, she could only scream. Paws thrust at her blouse, tearing it open. Instantly the creature released her and emitted a long, mournful howl— and dashed away, leaving her to spill onto the floor like a pudding. Packages of bread and hot dog buns cushioned her as she slumped helplessly against the shelves.

After a while Mollie began to hear moans, little clusters of *uh-uh-uh*s, over and over. She became aware of movement, of someone rocking back and forth, and of other sounds as the movement disturbed the clear plastic wrappers of the hot dog buns. Presently she came to accept that she herself was the one moving, and moaning. But neither stopped.

She sat on the linoleum, her left leg straight, right bent at the knee, ankle under her left knee. Something cold pressed against the bare skin of her right thigh: the empty tofu container, caught under her skirt. She pried it out and held it up to the light for examination. It seemed quite ordinary. But what was it doing out of the cooler?

And then she remembered: Oh.

The moaning stopped. She was not conscious of having stopped it. I should call the cops, she thought. I should report this. The decision taking shape, she thought about what she was going to say.

. . . The store out on Highway 90, that's right, just before you get to Moson Road . . . yes, a werewolf, that's what I said. It broke into the cooler and ate all the tofu . . . no, tofu . . . that's right . . . yes, a werewolf ate the tofu. And then it attacked me and tore my blouse, and ran away . . .

"OK," she muttered. "OK, I can't call the cops. I can't leave this mess for the midnight relief. Who's relieving me? Eldridge, right. I can't leave this for him. And I can't explain it to Carson, he'll fire me. So I have to clean it up, and hope they don't notice the loss during inventory week."

Slowly, like an accordion opening, she got to her feet. *Story of my life.*

* * *

Swing shift, Mollie told herself, wasn't all that bad. You got to sleep at night, and you had a few hours of daylight to enjoy before you went to work. It was better than having to sleep during the day and be up all night like a vampire.

Like a werewolf.

She slouched in front of the mirror in the bathroom of her efficiency apartment in the southern part of town. Except for the cross pendant, she was naked. In her recent memory she did not see herself driving home after Eldridge had relieved her, or climbing the stairs to the second floor of the apartment complex, or unlocking her door. Vaguely she remembered stripping off her clothes, because the light rustle of fabric across her nipples as she shrugged out of her blouse had given her the first sensation she could recall since she had stood and begun to clean up the mess around the cooler. She had also stepped out of her red plaid skirt and her undies.

So why are you in front of the mirror?

"I don't know," she answered herself, without enthusiasm. "Maybe because I'm the only one who wants to look at me." In the mirror she saw the bed behind her, and on it the teddy bear body pillow with one eye missing. In the light from overhead, the other eye seemed to be winking. "Except you, Claire," she said, seeking to reassure the teddy. Briefly the winking continued. For an instant she saw another shape there, and whirled around, mouth open for a scream. The teddy reformed, oblivious to its temporary transformation.

"No nightmares," she pleaded with it.

* * *

Stepping into a steam-filled shower stall always gave Mollie the feeling that she was a ghost, a spectral entity hidden—no, *trapped*—within her own contrived misty aura. Here she was safe, the outside universe reduced to vague images that broke through the steam here and there but never lingered long enough to reclaim her. The steam muted her senses. She was aware of the heat of the water without feeling it. The only sounds that reached her ears were consistent with the shower.

As for touch . . .

The experimentation had begun at fourteen, not long after her first period, and quite by accident. Touch had felt good, and more touch had felt even better, and the more thorough the touch, the more exquisite the sensation. The very first time, at the moment of peak sensation, she had started to scream, then choked it off, hoping her mother had not heard. After her breathing had slowed, and with her body still dripping lather and water, she had whispered, "Wow." Lately she had come to see that all of her wows had been marvels of solitary engineering. There had been several boys, but none with anything close to the skills that she herself had developed over the years. She had remained safe, clean, and alone.

For now, she forced herself to be content with allowing the shower to cleanse her of the day she had just passed. In the desert, water was expensive, and she did not earn enough to indulge too frequently. Where water was rationed, she had to ration herself. The caress of steam vapors would have to suffice.

Not until Mollie had finished drying herself did the realization break through the wall her subconscious was trying to erect: *I saw a fucking* were*wolf tonight.*

Still naked and somewhat damp, Mollie sat down on her bed, clasped her hands, and clamped them between her knees. Hunched over, she stared down at the small throw rug that cushioned her feet against the bare concrete floor. It had a design like a Native American talisman in turquoise and tangerine, but it could not defend her from the events of the evening. What did it mean, to see a werewolf? She had supposed the Dark Side to be something the entertainment industry invented, its creatures designed to chill and thrill, nothing more. Even now a part of her refused to credit what she had seen. Yet something had ripped her blouse. What, if not the creature?

She reached for the garment, which lay at the foot of the bed where she had cast it while disrobing. The top button was missing, and there were several tears on either side below the collar that rendered the blouse unusable, at least for work. She might wear it to putter around the apartment. It had cost her twenty-five dollars, and she had worn it perhaps half a dozen times. She could not charge a replacement to the convenience store.

Finally she stretched out on top of the bedcovers and reached for the teddy bear body pillow, drawing it close alongside her. She wrapped her arms around it, and draped her right leg over it. With her face pressed against the furry neck, she began to weep softly.

* * *

Morning arrived uninvited. Mollie threw an arm over her eyes to blot out the sunlight and rolled over, one leg draped over Claire. Dream sleep had not quite left her, and for a moment she experienced an erotic chill, as if she had not slept alone, after all. She murmured something unintelligible even to herself, and blinked rapidly, awakening at last.

"Gmorn, Claire," Mollie sighed, and disengaged herself from the body pillow. She sat up, dropping her feet to the rug. Scraggly straw-yellow hair spilled over her shoulders and breasts, giving her something of a Godiva look. *I'll bet*, she thought, getting to her feet, *I could ride a fucking horse through this town, dressed like this, and nobody would notice.* Cobwebs of sleep vaporized in the morning sunlight . . .

. . . and a dark shape flashed across her mind, a creature bristling with hair and teeth, ripping into her memory before it, too, vaporized.

"Jesus God!" cried Mollie. Eyes wide and wild, she looked around. Saw nothing to alarm her. Her arms felt strange. She raised her left, examining the forearm. The skin was covered with goosebumps, and all the fine pale hairs had come erect. "Jesus God," she whispered.

In a crisis, she thought, do something, anything. She moved to the old armoire in the corner by the window and rifled through it for panties, denim cutoffs, and a turquoise tee two sizes too large. Quickly she dressed, throwing on a pair of open-toed sandals for good measure, and went to the dinette for breakfast. The last of a box of muesli went into a bowl, followed by milk from the cooler, which, when she poured, emerged from the mouth of the bottle in clots.

Exasperated, Mollie poured the remains of the outdated milk down the kitchen sink, then stared out the window at the street alongside the apartment complex. As yet no one was stirring. Saturday, she remembered. *I am so not going to have a day like this,* she told herself firmly. She tucked a five into a front pocket of her denims and headed out for breakfast at the McDonald's down at the intersection.

* * *

Service was relatively quick at the McDonald's, Mollie being at the moment the only patron. She carried the tray with its two breakfast burritos, cake of hash browns, and cup of coffee to a table for two across the aisle from the bank of condiments, and sat down. In the background she heard a glass door open and close several times, but she did not look until she became aware of a dark shape in her periphery. She glanced up, and swallowed a scream.

The man standing just inside the side entrance might

have just emerged from her waking nightmare. On any other previous day she would have readily dismissed him as a bag man, but not today, not now. Mollie kept very still. He had not seen her yet. His narrow, pinched face and deep-set, bloodshot eyes were all but obscured by a thick mane of graying black hair. *Hasn't the man heard of razors*, she thought, and then banished the question from her mind before, as if he could hear her thoughts, he went off in search of one. *No sharp objects for him,* please!

Abruptly the man turned toward the rest rooms. Mollie stifled a hiccup of humor. *Do werewolves shave?*

A discussion slightly louder than the usual order-placement at the counter snagged Mollie's attention. Remonstrating with the cashier was a young woman attired in rags. Dumpster-diving-day for the bag people at McDonald's, Mollie thought. This one was wearing denim cut-offs rather like hers, but with the seams open all the way up to the beltline, revealing that she was either naked underneath or wearing a thong. A length of green and white bungee cord, tied in a bow in front, served as a belt. Above that, a tattered yellow tee covered the essentials of her upper body. It too was open along the flanks, the hem tied in knots on either side. Her feet were shod by a pair of shower clogs, the left clearly larger than the right, and the strap of the right one had popped loose, so that she had to crimp her toes to keep it on.

"There's nothing I can sell you for a quarter," the cashier repeated. "And you aren't dressed for . . ."

The woman indicated her feet and upper body. "Shoes plus shirt equals service," she said brightly.

The cashier defaulted to the primary objection. "But you have no money."

As the woman turned to leave, Mollie's eyes locked with hers. Face suddenly hot, as if she had been caught snooping in someone else's closet, Mollie averted her gaze, but before the moment could pass into oblivion, she looked at the woman once more, and on impulse made a little gesture toward the chair across the table. Without hesitation the woman accepted the offer. As she seated herself Mollie took a moment's smug satisfaction from seeing the cashier frown.

"Mollie," she said, extending her hand, and withdrawing it after a brief clasping during which she imprinted the woman's face in her mind. A shock of uncombed shoulder-length hair the exact color of freshly-sheared copper framed a heart-shaped, almost anime-like face dominated by wide, deep violet eyes. On that face, the snub nose seemed diminished. The anime similarity ended at the mouth, though. Instead of full-lipped, round and pouty it was wide and thin, the lower lip cracked here and there by the desert heat. Despite the ever-present Arizona sun her pale skin was unburned, albeit seriously freckled. All in all, concluded Mollie, as she withdrew her hand, it was not a beautiful face, but a face not to be forgotten.

"Short for Elizabeth?" asked the woman. Dryness lent a touch of smoke to her contralto.

Mollie cringed. "You wouldn't believe me even if I showed you my birth certificate."

"Perhaps not. But I wouldn't laugh, either. Oh, and I'm Claire."

The coffee cup in Mollie's hand paused halfway to her mouth. "Oh, but that's who I sleep with," she blurted, and almost dropped the cup on the tray. "Oh, jeez, I didn't mean to say that."

Claire brushed aside the *faux pas*. "That doesn't sound to me as if you're referring to your boyfriend."

"I don't have a . . . I mean, no, that's my teddy bear body pillow."

Shut up, Mollie. Shut up shut up shut up.

"I really don't need both these breakfast burritos," Mollie added quickly, fleeing the scene she had inadvertently created. "Impulsive of me, but I thought . . ."

Claire smiled. Heretofore Mollie had thought a smile capable of lighting up a room to be a Hollywood figment, but the table did brighten, as did her spirit. "I could make do with that, or half that slab of hash browns," said

Claire.

Mollie slid the tray to the middle of the table. After sniffing the burrito Claire took a big bite of it, hardly stopping to chew before she forced more into her mouth.

"I actually have money," said Claire, before swallowing. Her tongue flicked over her front teeth, scouring fragments of egg free. "I just neglected to . . . well, it's in my other clothes, along with my key. I have to call the landlord to let me in, and he won't be available until—what's wrong?"

"He's back," Mollie whispered hoarsely. "Jeez, he's back."

"He who?" Claire glanced at the counter, and turned back. "Oh. What about him?"

Feeling a chill, Mollie rubbed her bare arms, but said nothing.

"He scares you," said Claire. "He scared you?"

Mollie fought the urge to scramble to her feet and dash away. From the man, yes, but also from Claire, and from the embarrassment of having disclosed personal information, and from . . .

Mentally Mollie shook herself as a dog just out of the bath. From *herself*, she had been about to think. To flee from herself.

And from the knowing way Claire was looking at her. Mollie had no frame of reference for describing it, no one having quite looked at her in that way before.

What way?

Well . . .

As if Claire were a gardener and she were a freshly bloomed rose under her protection.

Mollie made a little sound of exasperation, and took a sip of coffee. *That sounds so*, she told herself, and stopped, unable to complete the thought.

"Mollie," Claire said softly.

Mollie blinked. "Sorry. Drifting."

The redhead grinned. "I've been known to do that."

"Yes," said Mollie. "He frightens me."

"Have you seen him somewhere before?"

Mollie hesitated. "I'm not sure . . ."

"Ah! He reminds you of someone that frightened you. Or—or some*thing*." Claire glanced at the man again. "Maybe you had a nightmare about werewolves or something. I can see how he might remind you of that."

Mollie just stared at her.

Suddenly there came the sound of impact, and Mollie started, with a little whimpered scream. The man had struck the counter for emphasis. "No, no *meat*!" he fairly shouted. "Just the green pepper. I can't have meat. I'm vegan."

"Looks more like he's from Arcturus," whispered Claire slyly. Mollie resumed her stare. "Hello?" added Claire, snapping her fingers. "That was a joke. You know. Joke?"

Exasperated, the man threw up his hands. "No! *Forget it!*" he yelled, and strode angrily out the exit.

"I don't think he means you any harm," said Claire. Her eyes went to the clock in the wall above the counter. "Oh, hey, I gotta make a phone call. Oh, wait, it's thirty-five cents. Damn!"

"We can go to my apartment," blurted Mollie.

Did I just say that?

Claire flashed a grin, then shook her head. "Not on the first date."

Mollie sputtered. "What? *Oh!* No, *no,* I'm not a—"

Before she could complete the clarifying protest, all thought came to a screeching halt. She had always supposed that to be a figure of speech, but now it seemed to her, as she listened to herself as if from a distance, that her brain was indeed grinding down, like a train pulling into the station. Metal wheels no longer rolled on metal rails, sliding now instead. The conductor in her frontal lobe set the handbrake. She was parked on a siding now. In a moment she could proceed, going back the way she had come, or . . .

Or.

The Universe had passed by on the main track, and now she was free to go. The brain fired up again, and its first act of cognition was

Oh
My
God

In slow motion, as if she were unaware of the act, Mollie set her coffee cup down on the table. Her eyes stared through Claire, through the great glass window that divided the eating bay from the playground outside, through the plastic Ronald, and the parking lot beyond, and beyond that the Superstitions and the Dutchman's yellow gold and on out to the farthest quasar.

Is that possible? How would I know? Whom can I ask?

Something hot and abrasive seized her wrist. Like a long telescope suddenly closing, she withdrew from the quasar, the Ronald, the window, *snap!*

"—all right?" Claire was pleading. "Hello?"

Mollie felt her irises focus.

Claire released her wrist and blew a sigh of relief. "*There* you are. For a moment there I thought you were someone else."

"Someone else," whispered Mollie. "Yes. Maybe . . ." She dragged weary fingers through her hair. "Oh, hell. I meant you could make a call from my place. It's not far."

"It's OK," Claire said gently. "I accept."

* * *

Mollie had expected Claire to follow her into the apartment, and was somewhat puzzled to turn around and find her still standing in the open doorway. During the ten-minute walk from the restaurant to her place, they had touched upon careers: Mollie had some interest in history and geology, which dovetailed rather nicely with Claire's background in anthropology and a fondness for spelunking and rockhounding, though neither woman had gone further than her junior year of college. By the time they reached the entrance to the apartment complex, they had touched upon current prospects, at which point Claire had become pensive. Now, at the top of the stairs, she had grown reluctant.

Mollie spread her arms in an unspoken question.

Claire's smile flickered. "I just recalled thinking that

you had become someone else," she said carefully. "And now I'm on the verge of entering your . . . lair, as it were."

"I was just . . . thinking, is all. Please. Come in."

Claire stepped into the room and closed the door behind her. "It must have been something I said, then."

Mollie's response was an absent whisper. "Yeah." She snagged the phone from its charging base and handed it to Claire. "I'm light on food, but I can probably find something more for you to eat."

"Doubtless," Claire said blithely. Punching out a number, she declined the offer with a shake of her head.

When she began speaking to her landlord, Mollie went to the dinette, to the window that looked onto the alley one floor below, and stood with arms braced against the sill, staring out in the general direction of the green dumpster. A part of her wondered what the hell she thought she was doing. Another part of her—

She knows the answers to your questions.

"But I don't know what to ask," Mollie muttered.

"A glass of water would be—" Claire called.

The abrupt end to the sentence made Mollie turn around. Claire had dropped the phone onto the bed and was doubled over, hugging herself.

"Bathroom!" she managed.

Mollie pointed, and Claire staggered in that direction. "No, the *other* door," said Mollie. "That's the closet. Are you OK?"

Presently from the bathroom came the sounds of retching. These passed. Mollie remained where she stood, as if nailed to the floor. The toilet flushed. Water ran in the sink. She heard spitting, and a sound not unlike that made when drinking water from a cupped hand. A brief silence followed, during which Mollie rather imagined that a towel was drying the redhead's face, mouth.

Mouth, thought Mollie.

She started when Claire emerged from the bathroom, pale and drawn. Dark streaks down the front of her ragged tee suggested water, not partially digested food.

"Sorry," Claire said weakly. "It must have been the sausage."

"I feel fine," said Mollie.

"Sausage prefers blondes," said Claire. "Um, the landlord will meet me in twenty minutes."

"Twenty minutes?" Mollie repeated, still a bit numb.

"Not enough time, sadly." She glanced around the room: at the unmade bed, at the armoire with the second drawer still open, at the dinette with a few dirty dishes on the counter. "Cozy place," she allowed.

"Not enough time for what?" Mollie asked.

"So that's Claire," said Claire.

Mollie moved to the bed and started to sit down, then thought better of it, as if something was lurking behind her, concealed within its own shadow, guiding her actions without explanation.

"So was it something I said?" pressed Claire.

"Grandma Moses," said Mollie. "Cornelius Vanderbilt."

In the dim light from the window Claire's eyes glistened with mirth like sparks from an amethyst crystal. She barked a laugh. "What?"

Mollie began to rearrange the two pillows at the head of the bed, making an inverted L with the Claire teddy. "Late bloomers," she explained. "Grandma Moses didn't realize she was an artist until she was like eighty. Vanderbilt didn't earn his first million until he was almost seventy."

"I see. So you think there's someone else inside you, trying to get out?"

"I don't think it's trying very hard," said Mollie, straightening the top sheet and the comforter.

"If you live in the dark, you do tend to blink at the first contact with light. Discovery is like that."

The simple statement shocked Mollie with its clarity. She stopped fiddling with the bed covers, but would not look at Claire. "You know what I'm talking about," she said, very softly.

Claire's tone contained a desultory shrug. "Life is discovery. Of who you could be. Whether that's also who you are, or who you become, is rather up to you. We all have potential."

Mollie nodded. "So what would you do if you thought you were on the verge of discovery?"

"Me? I'd run with it."

Mollie stood up, and looked at her at last. "Is that what you did?"

Claire grinned. "I'm Popeye. I yam what I yam. Hmm. Or is that Descartes?" She jerked a thumb at the door and began edging toward it. "Anyway, speaking of running, I must. Landlord, remember? Thanks for the . . . thanks for sharing."

"Wait—"

"Gotta go."

And she was gone.

* * *

All air left Mollie. She felt invertebrate as she collapsed, sitting, onto the bed, jostling the Claire pillow hard enough to make it almost sit up. Had she the strength, she would have wept. Instead, she clasped her hands and held them tightly between her knees, and hunched forward, fighting for breath. *Haugh, haugh, haugh.*

God what did I do?

What do I do?

Mollie slowly sat up.

She seemed interested in me as a person. As a friend. She knows I don't know where she lives. She knows where I live. If she is sincere, she will return.

"And what do I do then?" she asked the pillow.

The single eye merely winked at her, a reflection from the overhead light.

Her forearm, laid across her upper thigh, touched something crinkly, something hard. She slipped her hand into the pocket and found a dollar bill and a quarter and a dime and two pennies, the change from breakfast.

The coins should have been a quarter and three pennies. *There must have been a dime in the penny well,* she thought. *All lucky breaks appreciated.*

A dime I could have given her for her phone call, and not

invited her back here.

Mollie got to her feet and made for the dinette. "You're over-analyzing," she scolded herself. On the counter dirty dishes beckoned, and she dropped them one by one into the sink, the silverware last. After the forks landed she heard another metallic sound, and realized belatedly that it had come from the alley below. She peered out the window. The hairy man from McDonald's had thrown open the lid to the dumpster and was rummaging inside it.

Mollie's heart raced. Had he followed her home? Did he know she lived here? Even as those questions formed, he looked up at the windows, as if searching for something, and she ducked back before he spotted her. She wished she had curtains to draw, but there was no help for it, not now. She dashed to the door and closed the bolt and set the security chain. If the man changed into a werewolf, she doubted the measures would keep him out of her apartment, but he was not a werewolf yet.

Another *clang* reached her ears and she cringed. Perhaps he was frustrated by the poor pickings in the dumpster and had slammed the lid. What would he do next? Go door to door, checking for unlocked ones?

Mollie ran back to the dinette window and risked a peek. The man was not in the alley. She leaned closer to the window, to increase her angle of vision. Nothing. The alley was empty, save the dumpster and assorted detritus. Nothing moved. He was not there.

Oh God . . .

She could call the police. She could tell them . . . what? That a hairy homeless man was going through the dumpster in the alley behind her apartment? Oh, yes, they'd come right out for that.

Mollie growled in frustration. What to do?

She took a breath. She took several. She leaned on the counter and stared out at the alley and tried to relax. To think.

I could hit him with my Claire pillow.

Claire, she thought. She would know what to do.

No . . . she would expect me to know what to do. That's the kind of girl she wants.

She ran back to the door. Listened. Undid the chain and threw open the bolt. Cracked the door. Listened again. Nothing.

Wait. A knock? It came from downstairs. She heard voices. A man's voice, gruff and . . .

Girl she wants?

"Shhh!" said Mollie, listening carefully.

You said "girl she wants."

"Yes I did. Now be quiet. I'm busy."

A door banged shut. Presently she heard knocking again.

He was indeed going door to door, as she feared.

Mollie re-secured the door and returned to the bed to consider her options. The simplest was not to answer the door if he knocked. But if she did not answer, perhaps he would think that no one was home, that he might break in with impunity. As an alternative she might leave the apartment; if he broke in, he could do no harm to her.

"Lair," Claire had called her apartment.

Would she want a girl who would not defend her lair?

"Oh, she doesn't want me," said Mollie, with an air of finality. "Passing ships in the night. Or at McDonald's. What is that quote? Longfellow?" She thought for a moment. "'Only a look and a voice; then darkness again and silence.'"

It was the silence, she thought, that was the killer. The hairy man in the hallway below was as nothing compared to that silence. She'd had her look, bestowed upon her by the vivid Claire, and the voice as well, the little words and hints. She understood that now. The way Claire had looked at her. *What did she see that I cannot see?* The remark about first dates. Claire's sly retort at being offered something to eat. And . . . and that bit about there not being enough time. That *had* to mean—

"Omigod," whispered Mollie.

Claire had departed, hurriedly, and darkness had indeed returned, and silence.

Mollie closed her eyes. What would it be like? Touching her body the way she touched herself. Being touched the way she touched herself. But there would be so much more. Her mouth on mine, and on me. My mouth on her . . .

Mollie shivered, and rubbed fresh goosebumps on her arms.

"But how do I know that's what she wants? What if she was just being sassy?"

She had no answer for herself. She thought she caught a glimpse of something lucent in the back of her mind, but the knock at her door dispelled it. She swallowed a scream. *The kind of girl she wants would defend her lair.* So be it.

In the utility drawer next to the utensil drawer there was a small ball peen hammer she used for driving tacks into the wall, to hang pictures and calendars. Silently she drifted across the floor, opened the drawer, and withdrew the tool. The knock came again, more insistently this time. She waited, hammer raised and ready, without responding.

The doorknob jiggled. Again Mollie stifled a scream. Her knuckles whitened around the hammer's handle. She waited. She hoped to hear muffled sounds, of the man moving off down the hallway to the next apartment. Ears keened, she listened for knocking. Perhaps there was a series of fuzzy thumps; she could not be certain.

Mollie held her breath.

She kept very still, hammer aloft, eyes transfixing the door. Minutes took hours to pass. No more sounds reached her. Had the man left? She could not determine this unless she opened the door, and that entailed risk, a risk she did not have to take. Gradually the hammer descended. Her arm was growing weary, and the threat no longer felt imminent. Her lips parted to issue a sigh of relief. It was over, at least for the moment.

The hammer began to slip from her hand. She caught at it, and tossed it onto the old stuffed chair she had salvaged from a yard sale. Now it looked different, somehow: solitary, alone. *Single occupancy*, she realized. *I have a chair because I don't need a couch.*

She screamed at the peremptory knock at her door. In fright she forgot the hammer, but there was no time to remember it because as soon as her scream died she heard a voice in the hallway.

"*Mollie!* Are you OK? *Let me in!*"

Mollie dashed to the door, threw the bolt and chain and yanked it open. The shape of Claire seemed to materialize right there in the hallway. It was all Mollie needed to see. She glommed onto the redhead, throwing arms and legs around her. At first Claire staggered under the unexpected weight. Then she gathered herself and stepped into the apartment and kicked the door shut behind her, while Mollie cried into the side of her neck.

Gradually Mollie's feet lowered to the floor, but her arms remained in place, thrust around Claire's neck. She tried to stop crying, and gave up. She felt as if a fortress had surrounded her, the effect of Claire's embrace. With Claire in no apparent rush to disengage, Mollie stood there with her. Soon her respiration calmed.

. . . girl she wants.

Mollie took a step back. For a moment she closed her eyes, and opened them again, and nibbled at her lower lip. Claire shot her a puzzled look.

"The hairy man," said Mollie. She did not bother to dry her face. "He was here."

Claire's expression faded to neutral. "That's not why you withdrew from me."

Mollie hesitated. "I was frightened."

"Without fear, you would not possess the courage to overcome it," said Claire. She glanced at the hammer on the stuffed chair and added, "Besides, I think you can take care of yourself."

The redhead had changed clothes. Now she was attired in a short, green plaid skirt and a white jersey, and she had found a pair of tan sandals for her feet. She had also combed her hair and, probably, bathed. The faintest hint of Lady Stetson wafted from her. Belatedly Mollie realized that she had recognized Claire by her eyes, her anime face. It astonished Mollie to see that the brief but intense physical contact had hardened Claire's nipples. It astonished her even more to realize that she had in fact noticed this—and most of all, to realize that her own were in a similar state.

Jeez.

A smile toyed with the corners of Mollie's mouth. "Girl she wants."

"What?"

Face suddenly warm, Mollie shook her head quickly. "Nothing. You came back."

"I *had* to leave. But I didn't think we were finished."

"We?"

"You and I," Claire explained. "But I like 'we' better."

"Saves syllables, does it?"

After a stunned silence they both laughed. Then Claire said, the words blunt and direct, "That's not why you withdrew from me. The hairy man isn't here to be afraid of. You're afraid of the pronoun."

Mollie whispered, "Yes."

"Stand up straight."

"What?"

Claire began to broadcast orders in staccato. "And square those shoulders. Look me in the eye. Look the Universe in the eye. Say hello, Universe."

Mollie grinned, despite herself. "Hello, Universe."

"You slouch because your boyfriends have mostly been your height or shorter," said Claire. "I've seen it before. It's so unnecessary. Be you: if that's not good enough, neither are they. Sit down on the bed."

Mollie obeyed. "I don't know—"

"Who you are," Claire finished for her. "Yes, I saw that. Your moment of discovery. Your eureka. I told you what I would do."

"Run—run with it?"

"You want to know. You want to find out. I don't know why it has taken you all these years to discover yourself. A late bloomer, you said. So am I. I understand." Claire lowered her eyes to Mollie's tee. "I think you know your truth now. But it's only part of the truth. It's why I came back. May I sit down? There, beside you?"

Mollie's heart pounded. She braved a "Yes."

Claire plopped down on the edge of the bed, to Mollie's right, and twisted slightly to face her. She started to reach out, to take Mollie's hands, then thought better of it. "You showed compassion for a stranger in need," she said softly. "Your mind is stimulating, your intellect challenging. Despite struggling to make do, you have not given up. You have . . . sorry, what was that?"

"I asked you how you knew that," Mollie repeated.

"That you haven't given up?" Mollie nodded, and Claire went on, "The books in that bookcase. No cookie-cutter romances for you, nuh-uh. No, I see: histories. Orwell's *Down and Out in Paris and London*. A geology text—"

Mollie waved her hand dismissively. "I haven't read three-quarters of them."

"So you've read a quarter, then. Don't look at what you haven't done. Everyone has stacks and scads of stuff they haven't done. Look at what you've done, and then do more. Look at what you're going to do."

"What am I going to do?" Mollie wanted to know.

Claire paused. She gazed briefly down at the floor. "You said you had no boyfriends," she said quietly. "No lovers."

Mollie shook her head. "I never said that. I started to —but didn't quite."

"And the reason why not?"

Mollie fell silent for a moment. "They don't wow me," she said at last. "I suppose you're going to tell me that I haven't met the right wowwer yet."

"I don't have to. You just did."

"Oh, that is so fucking profound," snapped Mollie. She scrambled to her feet and moved away, and began to pace the floor in front of the armoire. Her voice grew louder as she vented. "You know so much about me. You know so much, period. So wise, you are. And I know what you are. I 'got' that bit about self-discovery. So yes, you had your big moment. But it's not that easy for others. For me. And how *can* you know so much? You're my age, right? How can you know all this about me and I don't even know it?"

"I'm twenty-four."

Mollie threw up her hands in disgust. "That's even worse. I'm three years older. What did I miss? What have I missed?"

"In some ways, I'm quite older," said Claire, still calm.

"More experienced, you mean."

"Yes, if you wish. Mollie—"

Mollie whirled on her. "Then where are *your* lovers? You have all this knowledge, all this experience. Where *are* they?"

Claire's eyes darkened, moist with regret. "They found out what I was, and left."

"That doesn't make any sense at all!"

"Mollie—"

"*What*?" Instantly she was contrite. "What is it?" she asked, her voice softer.

"You're still afraid of the pronoun. You are not truly vexed. You are reacting from fear."

Mollie sighed. "Yes. I am. And behaving badly. I'm sorry."

Claire patted the spot on the bed that Mollie had vacated. Mollie sat down, and folded her hands in her lap, and gazed down at the floor, and waited. For several seconds there was only the sound of their breathing. Dimly she was aware of the increase in body heat, and suspected that it stemmed from proximity rather than passion. The recent physical contact with Claire had been the result of fear and relief; sex had had nothing to do with it.

Even so, the contact had also brought her to the verge of arousal, and Claire as well. Their thin cotton shirts had been insufficient to conceal this fact. If that signified desire in Claire, then surely it signified the same for herself. More, when she had thrust her face against Claire's neck, there had been a momentary urge to kiss her there. From that point, it would have been a simple matter to shift her face around to Claire's, to touch lips with hers, and then to . . .

Mollie's chest heaved, and she shuddered with sparks that cascaded from her neck and shoulders and disappeared down her spine. Her groin stirred.

Oh dear God . . . I do . . . I am . . .

Mollie lifted her gaze to Claire. Neither spoke. Where before Claire had been bold and confident with her knowledge, now she looked placid, benign. She was waiting for something. Her distinctly non-anime mouth bore just a trace of a smile, the lips moist now and reflecting light from the overhead. Presently Mollie leaned closer, and almost lost her balance. To support herself she threw her right arm across Claire's shoulders, and scooted herself over the comforter. Claire's hands, clasped in her own lap, did not move. Seconds passed, and the gap narrowed between their faces as Mollie drew herself ever closer . . .

Can you hear my heart now?

—and closer. Warmth became heat. Mollie's nervousness refused to abate, so she ignored it. It was just as well, for in that moment their lips touched, and then there was only heat and heartbeats.

Mollie thought: *It's . . . different. It's like kissing—me, but not me.*

Then Claire's lips parted slightly, and Mollie stopped thinking altogether.

Scant seconds passed, and there came a moment when Mollie completely surrendered. She thrust herself against Claire, into Claire, her tongue a living thing now, Claire's darting past hers, then withdrawing, only to caress Mollie's and to suck on it, to draw it further into her mouth. Mollie lost her balance and slipped inadvertently from the bed to the floor.

And sat there gasping for breath.

Wow.

She felt Claire's hands on her arms, lifting, and a moment later she was back on the bed. Claire's eyes shone. Mollie rather imagined that her own did as well. She tried to find her voice, failed, and cleared her throat to try again.

"It might be well to take your necklace off," suggested Claire. "We don't want to tangle our hair." She dipped her fingers under her own jersey and fished out a fine golden chain with an amber cabochon pendant set in gold, and drew it over her head, clearing her hair. Mollie did the same with hers, and spilled it onto the night table. After Claire passed her the golden chain, the weight of it took her by surprise. She paused to examine it, hefting it in her hand.

"This," said Mollie, her voice husky now, "this is real gold."

"I know. I had it made."

"But—but this weighs . . . it must be a thousand dollars in gold."

Claire shrugged. "A bit more, I think."

"But—"

"I told you I had money, Mollie."

"But *this*—"

"Belongs on the night table," Claire said firmly, "next to yours."

"Yes. Yes, of course. There."

Claire spread her hand against Mollie's chest and gave her a gentle shove, sprawling her onto the bed on her back. While Mollie arranged her head on a pillow, Claire clambered further onto the bed and stretched out beside her, head resting on her left hand aprop her elbow. Her right index finger began to trace little designs on Mollie's jersey, just over her sternum.

"You snogged me," said Claire.

"Sorry. Won't happen again."

Claire pouted, and Mollie added, "Or will."

Mollie felt Claire's fingertip expand its tracing to include the inner swells of her breasts.

"So what is Mollie short for?" asked Claire.

"My Dad was a high school chemistry teacher," said Mollie. "And very eccentric."

Claire began tracking her finger down now, toward Mollie's navel. In sprawling onto the bed, the tee had ridden up, and Mollie expelled a puff of air at the contact with her bare skin. Tiny muscles fluttered on her abdomen, as if a flock of butterflies had landed there.

"So?" prodded Claire.

"Molybdena," said Mollie. "Female form of molybdenum. Or so he supposed."

Mollie felt Claire's finger—fingers, now—pass over the front of her cutoffs, and down the top of her right thigh. For a moment she was in her shower, lathered up. But it was not quite the same. This was not her own practiced touch, but the touch of—another woman.

What am I doing?

"Molybdena," repeated Claire, savoring each syllable. "Oh, I quite like that. Hmm. Very high melting point, molybdenum. Let's see if that's true." She withdrew her hand. "Close your eyes."

Mollie obeyed. "What are you going to do?"

"What do you want me to do?"

"Oh, that's not fair! I don't know—"

"Close your eyes."

". . . I don't know anything about . . . I don't know how . . ."

"Shh! We're women. We aren't built for invasive, penetrating love-making. We aren't takers. We aren't built for taking what we want. We're givers. I give to you, you give to me. I make you wow, and you make me wow. We give to each other. That's how it works best. Touch is our guide. We respond to it. The response tells us we're doing something right. You touch yourself, right?"

"Well . . . yes."

"Keep your eyes closed. You wow yourself?"

"It's the only—"

"Shh. I understand. It's OK. But given a choice, wouldn't you prefer that I did that for you? That I gave that to you?"

"But you aren't even touching me now—" And she gasped, a prolonged expulsion of air, as Claire's fingertip unexpectedly passed with a feather's caress across her left nipple. It came erect instantly, and in the same moment Mollie arched her back. The gasp finished, she collapsed back onto the bed.

Presently Mollie opened her eyes. The sensation of unexpected contact had left her bereft of thought. If Claire had placed two paddles against her body and yelled, "Clear!" she could not have elicited a greater response.

"Never," she sighed, not quite speechless.

"It's not something you could do to yourself," Claire pointed out. "You always know where your hand is."

"I can do without the analysis of technique."

Claire laughed. "Sorry. Just one more observation: you were named for the wrong element. I believe gallium melts at room temperature."

Mollie was inclined to agree, but said nothing as Claire's hand resumed its tracing, its journey. Once more she closed her eyes, and set her senses adrift. To relax utterly she spread-eagled herself, her arms crossing the T of her body. Her left hand smacked against the top of the nightstand, jostling the necklaces. The impact distracted her from Claire's touch.

My tee completely conceals my necklace. How did you know I was wearing one?

"Are you all right?" asked Claire. "For a moment there, you tensed."

"I hit my hand."

Claire leaned across Mollie and drew the injured hand to her lips, kissing it gently before setting it back down. "Better?"

With Claire's breast pressed over her mouth, Mollie could only mumble a response. The contact itself was stunning, and Mollie's right hand twitched as she stifled the urge to slide it under Claire's jersey.

As if reading Mollie's thoughts, Claire sat back on her haunches, grasped the hem of her jersey with both hands, and drew it up over her head, casting it to the foot of the bed. Her tan suggested she had worn a loose tank top on occasion, but only rarely a bra. Her breasts, like Mollie's, were not much larger than average oranges; she scarcely required any support.

"Your turn," said Claire.

Mollie hesitated. "I'm not sure I'm . . . ready to . . . to . . ."

"Take your top off? It's just like the showers in high school gym class, right?"

"That's . . . that was different."

"True." Claire laid back down and propped her head on her hand again. "I'm sorry. It's new to you. You've never been naked and sexual with another woman. You want to be . . . but at your own speed, your own time."

"I'm sorry. I'm . . . just not ready to take my clothes off."

"Well . . . I had hoped to assist you with that. Don't want you doing all the work."

Mollie laughed, despite herself.

"And don't be sorry," added Claire. "At least you haven't asked me to leave."

"I would never—" began Mollie, and froze. She had reached for Claire to reassure her, and instead palmed her breast, almost cupping it, her fingers slipping between Claire's flank and arm. Before she could withdraw from contact, Claire pressed her upper arm against Mollie's hand, securing it there.

"If you do not wish to touch me," said Claire, "I'll release you."

Mollie swallowed. "All right. I mean, no, it's OK." On impulse she took a chance, moved her thumb, brushed it across the nipple, which was pebbly now. Claire drew a breath and leaned into Mollie's palm, and made a tiny sound, half-growl, half-yum.

It was almost, but not quite, the same sound Claire had made while eating the burrito. Which had not stayed down. She had blamed the sausage.

But mine was OK.

Mollie pulled her hand away.

Claire's eyes widened. "What is it? What's wrong?"

The possibility that had just flown through Mollie's mind vanished before she could hold it down for examination.

That doesn't make any sense at all!

I said that earlier. Because Claire had said her lovers had found out who she was.

But wouldn't they have already known?

The hard knock at the door startled them both. Claire's hand moved with dazzling quickness to cover Mollie's mouth, while Mollie went rigid with fear.

"Shh," hissed Claire, the sound just audible.

Mollie nodded, and Claire removed her hand. It's him, Mollie mouthed.

The doorknob rattled, but remained locked. They turned their heads to stare at it. Claire sat up, then pulled Mollie up.

"You didn't do the chain!" Mollie whispered hoarsely. "Or the bolt!"

Claire twisted off the bed and knelt on the floor, dragging Mollie to her knees to face her. Hands vised Mollie's arms, and she almost cried out.

"Listen to me," said Claire, her lips moving against Mollie's ear, her voice fierce. "I will never, ever harm you. Understand?"

"N-no . . ."

"*Ever*! And I will never let anyone harm you. Believe that."

Mollie did not move.

"Please, Mollie." She sounded almost in tears. "*Believe* me. *Trust* me. I do not want another lover to leave me. I do *not* want to lose *you*."

Something thumped against the door. Mollie heard a splintering sound. She stiffened in fear. "Claire," she breathed. "It's the hairy man. He's a werewolf."

"No," said Claire. She stood up, and took a few steps back. "He's not."

At the next impact, the door began to give, but Mollie now paid no attention to it. Before her eyes, Claire's hair grew and darkened, her face elongated and her mouth filled with a carnivore's teeth. Her body changed, darkened, the breasts atrophied to nothing more than nipples, the elastic band that secured the green plaid skirt expanded almost to breaking, the sides of the sandals split open and their straps tore apart.

Frozen on her knees on the floor, Mollie screamed. The door yielded. The hairy man burst into the apartment. His eyes found the armoire immediately, then grew huge as Claire stepped into his view. He started to flee, and was snared by a pair of massive paws. Claire thrust him against the wall, and kicked the door shut.

It shocked Mollie to learn that Claire had a voice in this form. She spoke carefully, deliberately, in one of those deep artificial voices Mollie had heard on scifi shows. "If you ever return, if you ever tell anyone what you saw here, *I will hunt you down and rip you apart.* Do *not* nod your head at me. I do not require your understanding, only your departure." She threw the door open again. "Go! *Now!*"

The man dashed down the hallway. The echoes of his footsteps faded.

Mollie wanted to scream again, but could not make a sound. She knelt on the floor by the bed, gaping like a beached trout. She felt like a pudding. She hadn't the strength or the will to climb back onto the bed, or to prevent herself from spilling onto the floor.

At the sound of impact Claire dropped to all fours, tail protruding from her skirt, and padded over to Mollie, where she whimpered, and licked her face. White showed all around Mollie's jade irises. She wanted to withdraw from Claire's ministrations, yet dared not move.

"I promised you," whispered the werewolf.

"Goway!"

Tears formed in eyes still purple. "All right."

Claire loped away, to the floor in front of the armoire, and laid down. Presently her body shrank, the hair withdrew into the body, the nails into the wolf toes and the wolf toes became human toes and fingers. The head shortened and broadened, the hair lightened once more to copper. At the end, only the eyes remained unchanged.

With a huge effort Claire stood up, kicked the burst sandals from her feet, and retrieved the jersey from the bed, while Mollie shrank back from her, and finally collected herself enough to crawl onto the bed, never taking her eyes off Claire.

The werewolf tilted her head, as if considering what to say and whether to say it. Cautiously she approached Mollie, and dropped to her knees beside the bed, and leaned her upper body onto the comforter as if in supplication. She did not touch Mollie.

"For me," she said gently, almost pleading, "it has always begun with a bit of lust. Love takes longer. It means learning to accept flaws, it means learning to trust . . . it means caring. Last night, in your store, I found you attractive as well as brave. That was the lust. I was going to . . . well, to lick you. Then I saw . . ." Her eyes went to the chain on the nightstand. With great care to avoid contact with Mollie's she retrieved the golden one and draped it around her neck.

"Silver," whispered Mollie.

"I'm very sensitive to it."

"I shouldn't wonder," Mollie muttered.

"So I start with lust," Claire continued. "It's never lasted long enough to transform into love. I've begged and pleaded, but no one could . . . stand me, not after they saw . . . what else I was. It's funny. You understood the concept of being 'someone else,' so I wondered whether you knew, or at least suspected. But you never said definitely."

"I thought you were talking about . . . your orientation."

"I realize that, now. Mollie . . . you've only just discovered yourself. The hardest part is *allowing* yourself to learn. With me, I hope. With me. Like I said, previously it's never lasted long enough. But I truly think, in time, *this* time . . . Mollie, I could love you."

"Me and a vegan werewolf," muttered Mollie.

"I was vegan before the change. You keep your attitudes, your gender, your . . . orientation."

"How did . . . ?"

"Short version? I was rockhounding in the Superstitions. I found a fissure in the rocks, and slipped inside to investigate. I was attacked. When I came to, I found myself among all these rotting burlap sacks of nuggets and dust."

Mollie sat up straight. "You found *The Dutchman's Lost Mine?*"

"I didn't see his name anywhere. But yes, I suppose so. I have to be careful, not to spend too much at one time, but . . . but it doesn't matter right now. I'm sorry to have frightened you, Mollie. But I meant every word I said to you."

Claire pushed herself up, and stood.

"Where are you going?" Mollie asked.

"Where do you want me to go?"

Mollie sat looking up at her for a long time. If asked, she could not have said what or even whether she was thinking. Glimpses of flashbacks passed in review in her mind, without drawing comment from her. She felt, rather than saw. There was a lot of fear, most of it fear of the unknown. As the flashbacks came to an end, she wondered whether she was afraid of the werewolf or of the love. It was easy to say both. But it was just as easy to say neither.

"Nowhere," answered Mollie.

Claire inclined her head in acknowledgement. It seemed to Mollie that her expression was one of immeasurable relief.

"We have some things to work out," said Mollie. "Where we live—"

"Your place," said Claire. "Mine's a dump."

"And where we work—"

"Quit your job," said Claire. "We'll travel, explore."

"And discuss things before making decisions," said Mollie, with some asperity.

"Sorry. It's a big change, for both of us," said Claire.

"We have time."

"And find you some sort of elastic wardrobe."

"Not spandex. It tends to fly apart like a grenade."

"But first—"

"First, if you don't mind, I'm going to take a shower," said Claire. "Right after a transformation, I usually smell like a wet dog."

"I was just going to suggest," allowed Mollie.

As steam began to filter out of the bathroom, Mollie assembled from her closet some clothing she thought might fit Claire, at least until she could retrieve her own from her "dump." Mollie's head filled with odd thoughts, about dietary changes and adjustments, about going back to college, about where to cache spare clothing. Gradually it occurred to her that she was avoiding the one subject she truly ought to be thinking about.

Cautiously, almost timidly, she went into the bathroom. Wraiths of steam gathered around her, the territory familiar to her, and she relaxed. On the other side of the frosted doors she saw a pixellated pink-tan silhouette splotched here and there with globs of soapsuds. She cleared her throat for attention. "I could scrub your back," she offered.

"Won't that mean you have to take your clothes off?"

It did.

002: A Spanner in the Works

Turbulence upset Mollie's stomach. She'd supposed that seats in first class would be less susceptible to it, but such was not the case. Already she'd spilled a third of her Tequila Sunrise onto the drop-down tray. Beside her, gazing out the window at the trickle of water in the Colorado River far below, Claire scarcely noticed the disturbance.

Presently Claire's hand reached over and took Mollie's. Neither woman spoke, nor did they have to. Mollie calmed herself, and soon began to peer past Claire at the stretch of dry terrain.

"Full moon tonight," whispered Mollie.

The redhead merely nodded, and gave her hand a squeeze.

"Our first together," Mollie added.

"I do feel the pull, that much is fair to say," Claire admitted, smothering a yawn. "But whether I change is still up to me."

"There goes another myth."

Claire laughed. "Folks who advance myths are usually trying to sell you something. We're just like you. We have the same feelings, the same needs." With a wicked grin she added, "Plus one or two you probably don't have."

Mollie blushed, but said nothing.

"What on Earth are you two talking about?" asked a woman in the seat behind them.

Mollie peered over the seat. The woman was in her fifties, with a mouth set in perpetual censure. Already her hair was completely gray, and fixed tightly to her round head with small brown combs. Her blue eyes, as dark as the plain-cut blouse she was wearing, registered disapproval.

Irritated, Mollie said, "My companion is a werewolf. We were just reviewing her finer qualities."

"There's no need for you to be rude, young lady,"

snapped the woman.

Mollie rolled her eyes, and turned back around. Claire said softly, "You shouldn't have told her that."

"We land in ten minutes," Mollie replied defensively, in the same tone. A flip of her hand sent her long yellow hair back over her shoulder. "We'll never see her again."

The whine of the engines as the plane began its descent toward Eugene drowned out Claire's response. *Great*, thought Mollie. *I've upset her.* A downcast expression swept over her; she stared at her knees and folded her hands in her lap. *She's right: I need to be more careful about what I say.*

"I'm sorry," Mollie said. "I'll try not to do that again."

"I growl—er, grouched, too. It's that time of the month."

"Ah. PMS."

Claire laughed, and flicked a glance meaningfully out the window port. "The *other* month," she said.

"Is it—? I mean . . ."

"We'll talk in the car on the way to Florence."

"Why Florence?" Mollie had asked, two days earlier, at breakfast.

Claire shrugged. "No particular reason. The nearest airport is in Eugene. We'll rent a car and head for the coast. Florence is just the closest city there."

"You've been there before," Mollie realized. But she'd put a little edge to her tone.

Claire kissed her, and nuzzled her cheek. "Not with someone else, *p'tite*. At least, not in the sense you mean."

"That sounds ominous," Mollie said darkly.

"Yeah."

Mollie winced. "Sorry. Past is past; now is now."

"Now is we, you and I. So is tomorrow. Finish your croissant."

"It still sounds ominous," said Mollie.

Claire tapped an index finger on the table top. Finally she said, "We do things. I've done things. Or I did until I learned control. Some of us have regrets."

"*Je ne regrette rien.*"

Claire nodded. "Edith Piaf—I regret nothing. There's a statement to the effect that all the things we do are nothing more than waypoints in our lives, and lead directly and inexorably to this moment in time. If, at this moment, we are where we were meant to be, and doing what we were meant to do, then the past, however negative, does not signify."

"You were meant to be a werewolf?" asked Mollie, incredulous.

"And your lover," Claire said solemnly.

"I thought we made our own fate."

Claire got up and began clearing the table. "Yes, we're destined to do that."

"You're arguing in circles to avoid telling me why we're going to Florence."

Claire paused, and turned to face her. "One of us has deep regrets," she replied. "And has posted on Farcebuch that he intends to, as he put it, 'come clean.' Fortunately, he has kept his secret, so far. But I know Travis, and I know what proof he will provide to clinch his claim."

"Omigod," cried Mollie. "And on national television, I'll bet."

"There will be those viewers," Claire said calmly, "who will attribute the transformation to computer graphics, not an unreasonable conclusion. But others will wonder, and speculate. If HomeSec becomes involved . . . the possibilities are unthinkable."

"They would try to weaponize you," said Mollie, her voice filled with horror.

"Literally me," agreed Claire. "Travis will name names. One of them will be mine."

Conversation in the Denali on the way from Eugene to Florence passed lightly. Mollie, who had never traveled further west than Tucson, watched slack-jawed as Highway 126 wove its way through mountain passes, crossed the Siuslaw, and charged headlong through forests she had only seen in Nature programs. Here indeed was a proper terrain for a werewolf, as well as for wolves in general. It made Mollie wonder why Claire, who had been here before, would ever have returned to the dusty desiccation of southeastern Arizona. She gave voice to her curiosity.

"I had to meet you, *p'tite*," was Claire's explanation.

"Seriously."

Claire braked a little as they spotted a deer near the road shoulder. To Mollie's relief, it shied away.

"I told you," said Claire. "Waypoints. Or karma, if you like. I told you I had done . . . things. But I learned from them, from the so-called error of my ways."

"You've killed people?" Quickly Mollie averted her eyes. Her hands occupied themselves by smoothing a couple of wrinkles in the thighs of her blue jeans. "I didn't mean . . . I hadn't asked, and . . ."

Claire smiled tolerantly. "I would kill to protect you, *p'tite*," she told Mollie. "Or die, if need be."

Mirth made Mollie giggle—a sound she thought she had outgrown. "I'm not really petite," she said. "I'm five-eleven."

"Calling you *grande* instead of *p'tite* takes the romance out of it." She touched the brake again. The blue pickup behind her honked in protest, then swung around, the driver gesticulating. A rifle rested in a rack in the rear window. "Mind that bridge abutment," Claire called out in return, through the closed window, and sighed. "I try not to hit animals. Like that squirrel."

"I would never criticize."

The redhead patted Mollie's thigh. "I know you wouldn't. Where was I?"

"Karma."

"I think that's a town in Illinois." She drew a slow breath, and let it out, puffing her lips. "Sometimes it bites you in the afterlife," she went on. "But other times, if you learn from your mistakes and make the proper adjustments, karma forgives you. I needed some money to set up a trust fund, a college fund, for . . . a child. Which meant I had to return to the Superstitions."

"I think I understand," said Mollie.

"I think you do. And . . . thank you for not asking."

Claire focused on the road, and Mollie made her a gift of silence. Minutes later, Claire broke it.

"I have more than enough money," she assured Mollie. "But it's wise not to keep it all in one place. I have a very well-paid accountant who handles finances for me, provided I give him something to handle." She barked a laugh. "Okay, I could have phrased that better. I meant gold, and cash."

"H-how much are we talking here?" asked Mollie. It was one thing to be able to rent a Denali for two weeks without so much as blinking. What Claire was referring to was something far else.

"At the current rate for gold?" She made a face. "Mollie, the Dutchman was very busy for many years. A couple of decades, I'd guess. And the vein did not run out; there's more. The dust and nuggets probably will add up to . . . oh, maybe two hundred million."

"Holy Hannah's herniated hatbox, Batman!"

Claire deepened her voice. "That's right, Robin. It's a tidy sum." She went on in her smoky contralto. "I've gotten about half of it out and secreted here and there or converted anonymously to cash. That anonymity requires that I take a bit of loss on the conversion, no questions asked. As I said, my accountant does not want for anything. So: I set up a trust fund. That was over four years ago."

"You had just turned twenty when it . . . happened?"

"Nineteen, when I killed the boy's father." At Mollie's sharp intake of breath, she added, "Yes, I can say it. I don't like it, but I can say it. I've faced myself. I'm better than I was. And now I have you in my life."

Mollie strained against the seat belt to kiss Claire's shoulder. "Always."

Suddenly Claire braked hard, and swung onto the shoulder, the tires skidding in gravel before they reached the grass. The man who had passed them in frustration earlier now stood in a roadside picnic area a hundred yards ahead, with his rifle aimed in their general direction.

"Turn around," Mollie suggested, her voice taut.

Claire put the Denali into park, and shook her head. "He'll just hurt someone else," she replied. "For all he knows, we could have an infant in the back seat. He doesn't care. He's irritated, he has power in the form of a rifle, and he's going to express himself with it. Besides, who's going to witness our murders? If a car comes along, he'll simply wait until it clears. No, *p'tite*, he's a danger to everyone, and he has just now announced himself. The Law won't prevent him from killing us. Oh, it might seek and obtain what it thinks of as justice, but we'll still be dead. So would the woman with the baby in the back seat."

Claire grasped the door handle and started to pull it. A touch from Mollie stopped her. Their eyes locked, violet on jade. Mollie averted hers. Claire said, "He can't kill me. And I've been shot before."

She exited the SUV before Mollie could counter with another argument. The man raised the rifle and sighted just as Claire dove into the gully that ran alongside the road. A pair of reports sounded, but the bullets passed harmlessly. Mollie's heart thudded. The man was serious. Claire was in trouble. Mollie knew she was transforming, but that wouldn't be enough. A distraction was needed.

Mollie threw open the passenger-side door and dove out. Before the man could fire again, she scurried around behind the Denali. Her breaths came ragged now, but there was no time for calm. She scooted to the driver's side, took a deep breath, and stepped out into the open, waving her arms.

"Here!" she called. "Here!" And she dove back behind the vehicle.

More shots rang out. One ricocheted off the gravel and went screaming into the woods. Another rang off the pole that held up the Rest Stop sign. After about a ten-second lull, Mollie tried it again. This time one of the bullets grazed the top of her left shoulder. She cried out, and ducked behind the car.

The wound was not serious, but did draw blood. It trickled down onto her tank top, the red a sharp contrast to the aqua fabric. A lull followed, broken this time by a flurry of shots and a horrible scream that ended abruptly. Mollie risked a look. The man was lying on the ground, with a long lump of black fur beside him that was Claire. Neither was moving.

Mollie started to run toward them, and realized the Denali would be quicker. She skidded to a stop only a few yards away from them, and shot out of the vehicle. Stumbling on the gravel, she spilled headlong onto Claire's hind legs.

The man's throat had been torn out. He was still alive, but burbling. Mollie ignored him. She jostled Claire, trying to rouse her.

The eyes that looked up at her had remained violet despite the transformation. There was no pain in them, only a hint of affection and of concern. "You shouldn't have," she breathed, in the low slow voice of the werewolf.

"I couldn't...I couldn't..."

A bloody paw touched her arm. "I know. Oh, you're hit!"

"A scratch." Mollie gave her a quick examination. "Claire, you've been shot."

"Tell...tell me about it."

Her hands fluttered. "But what do I do? I don't know what to do."

"It's complicated."

Mollie helped her up, setting her on all four feet. Blood dripped from Claire onto the gravel of the road shoulder. Mollie fretted over that, wringing her hands. If Claire's DNA should be identified...and what would it show? Human or werewolf, or some combination? There was no way for her to protect Claire.

The werewolf paused, and gestured with a paw. "I left my clothing over there," she said, her voice returning almost to the contralto.

Mollie went to gather it up. When she returned to the

spot, Claire was already on the passenger seat, her nose out the window sniffing the air. Mollie climbed in and started the vehicle, and took off with a spray of gravel behind them. Soon enough, someone would come along and spot the body and the pickup. An all-points bulletin would be issued. She drove along the road as fast as she dared. The Denali was an excellent vehicle, and clung to the pavement as if it were on rails. An oncoming car accelerated her heart rate and respiration. Discovery might well be imminent.

"You said complicated," she prodded Claire, catching her breath. "I-I...aren't you in pain?"

"Some," Claire conceded. "That's not the problem. I have three bullets in me. One is lodged next to my heart."

"Oh my God!"

"It won't kill me," she said quickly. "Bullets can't kill a werewolf. But it means I can't transform back to my human form until I've healed."

"Oh my God!"

A paw caressed her knee. "Calm yourself, *p'tite*. I need you clear-headed. Can you do that for me?"

Mollie swallowed hard, and nodded.

"Good. I heal very quickly. I've actually had a bullet in my heart before. Some rancher...well, it can wait. But I must stay awake in order to hold back the transformation process. If I should fall asleep..."

"You can't, oh God, you can't."

"Mollie."

She drew a huge breath and let it out slowly, in shuddering puffs. "All right," she said. "All right. What do you need me to do?"

"Stop at the next convenience store," answered Claire. "Park around the side, where the cameras won't pick up the car. Go inside and buy about three of those five-hour energy drinks. And for good measure, get yourself a soda."

Laughing nervously, Mollie started the SUV and drove off.

The road meandered a little, and finally straightened as

it came down from the last of the foothills. At an intersection with a north-south road stood a gas mart and a small restaurant. Following instructions, Mollie parked well to one side, although no security cameras were in evidence. Before leaving the Denali she tousled her hair and tore her tank top. She adopted a slovenly manner to her carriage, as if she didn't give a damn about anything or anyone, and entered the gas mart.

The clerk at the cash register was a gangly youth in a red and black checked flannel shirt and blue jeans, and his brown hair was in even worse condition than Mollie's. A set of earphones said he was paying scant attention to customers as he rocked his body back and forth. More relaxed now, Mollie ignored him, and bought a six-pack of drinking water, a soda, and the energy drinks Claire had requested. She started to pay with plastic, thought the better of it, and dug the cash out of her wallet. The clerk shifted gears, made and gave her change, bagged the smaller items, and resumed rocking back and forth.

Caught a break there, thought Mollie, departing.

Claire seemed worse off than before. Her breathing was ragged and shallow, and she was drooling, some it of tinged with red. Mollie moaned in sympathy.

"What can I?" she began, and spread her hands helplessly. "Oh, Claire, I don't...don't know what to do for you."

"It's all right, *p'tite*," the werewolf replied weakly. "I just need time. Open one of those energy drinks for me, would you?"

Mollie did so. "How are you going to drink it?"

"Pour some in the cup of your hand. I'll lap it up."

Claire drank one can, spilling but a few drops, and slumped in the passenger seat, panting. Mollie shot her a worried look, but said nothing as she drove back onto Highway 126. Silence concerned her; noise would help Claire stay awake. Mollie turned on the radio and scanned for FM channels, and found one that played rock oldies. Led Zeppelin's "Immigrant Song" was on, and she turned the volume up to a point where it matched her conversational voice.

"I would rather just talk," said Claire, and Mollie lowered the volume to threshold.

"We're coming up on Tiernan," said Mollie. "There might be a motel where we can stay for a couple of days. Hmm...I wonder if they take pets."

Claire laughed, and then whimpered. A hard, worried look from Mollie made her stop, take a deep breath, and find a smile. "Not at Tiernan," she said. "Once that body is discovered, the nearest small towns are the first places the police will look."

Mollie looked glum. "I hadn't considered that."

"This road meets up with Highway 101 in Florence," Claire said calmly. "Take it north to Heceta Beach. Maybe there are motels; we'll try one."

"Just stay awake," mumbled Mollie. "That's all I ask: just stay awake."

"I'll be just fine," Claire assured her. "It helps that there's a full moon."

They were less than five miles from Florence when two police cars and an ambulance rushed by them on their way east. Mollie slowed and pulled the Denali to the side of the highway, as prescribed by law, but none of the emergency vehicles paid the slightest attention to them. When they passed from the rear-view mirror, she returned to the road. Beside her, Claire was panting. Mollie fished around for a tissue, and wiped at Claire's lower jaw.

"Sorry," said Claire.

"Are you...in any pain?"

"I have a mantra: I'm a tough werebitch."

Mollie smiled, despite her fears. "Is it working?"

"No."

After they passed through a sparse pine forest, Florence came into view. Mollie used the vehicle's WiFi to search for motels in Heceta. The closest motels were in north Florence. "There's a small place off the highway, about two miles north," Claire told her. "Bunga-Low. They have about a dozen units, no questions asked.

Mexican berry pickers stay there during season."

Mollie shook her head. "I don't see that one listed."

"You won't. And watch the road!"

"Sorry."

"It's too bad we're not here in May," said Claire. "We could see the Rhododendron Festival." Suddenly she pointed. "There! You can see the bridge across the Siuslaw River. It looks like a miniature Bay Bridge."

"Our turn's coming up."

They merged into light Highway 101 traffic, and watched for the Bunga-Low as they made their way north. At just over two miles out, they spotted the motel and its train of units off to the right, and took that exit. Moments later, Mollie pulled the Denali alongside the office, where it could not be seen, and told Claire to stay down while she went inside to register.

As Claire had said, no questions asked. Mollie paid in advance for three days, filled out a paper with as much false information as she could, once she learned that the clerk required no identification. The only factual entry she made was the Denali's license plate number, because that could readily be verified simply by walking by the vehicle.

Finished, Mollie stepped outside and breathed a sigh of relief. She drove a short distance to Unit 14, the last one in the train, got out, and unlocked the door. After a quick check to see that no one was outside looking, she waved Claire into the unit, and quickly shut the door.

"Safe," said Mollie. She frowned at the trail of red droplets on the threadbare pea-green carpet. "Claire?" she said weakly.

The werewolf shook her head. "I popped a scab, getting out of the car," she said. She sat on her haunches, and curled her muzzle to one of the wounds to lick at it. Satisfied, she added, "You'd better get something to eat. I saw a vending machine in the alcove by the office."

"I-I can't leave you, Claire. What if you fall asleep?"

"Just go."

Mollie went. She did not dawdle, but neither did she move so swiftly that she risked attracting attention. The soda machine accepted both cash and plastic. Not wanting to leave an unnecessary trail, she slipped in a pair of ones. Another pair went into the vending machine. She returned to the unit with the soda, a bag of chips, and a candy bar.

"Nourishment," Claire said drily.

Mollie sank into a chair and tore open the bag of chips, sending several flying. "How are you feeling?" she asked, as Claire munched from the floor.

"I should have another energy drink."

She got one out and opened it, and poured some into her cupped hand. After Claire finished the bottle, Mollie stretched out on the bed, hands folded under her head, worried and disappointed. Soon helplessness depressed her even lower. She felt she ought to help Claire in some way; bandages, perhaps, or a compress, or think of a way to remove the bullets.

"Did they go through?" she asked abruptly, as the possibility occurred to her.

The werewolf managed a bleak, brief smile. "In and out." She laid down on the carpet, but kept her head erect.

Mollie picked up the remote and turned the television set on. Scrolling through the menu, she found only two dozen channels—the basic programming from cable. "Ooo, *As the Stomach Churns*," she said, with mock gusto. "We can find out whether Nora has told Dirk about Spike. Hmm...the SyFy channel has—you won't believe this—*An American Werewolf in London*. Is that an omen, or what?" Her smile faded; she was becoming hysterical, prattling nonsense."

"Take a deep breath," Claire advised. "Mollie...no, look at me, Mollie. I'm going to be all right. I just need a few more hours."

"It will be dark in two," said Mollie.

"And the Moon will be full."

"I could call Travis," she offered. "Maybe he can help."

"I don't want to let him know I'm in the area yet. Speaking of which, see if you can get the local news. Try

KMTR; that's in Eugene."

"And...got it. Six o'clock news. You don't suppose..."

"That's what I want to find out."

They watched: news, weather, sports. A blue-chip quarterback had signed a letter of commitment to the Ducks. A storm was approaching the coast, and might deposit two inches of rain before it swept over the mountains. The senior senator was coming all the way from Washington, D.C. tomorrow to explain why he had cast the deciding vote in favor of new, top secret, research and development of alternative defenses.

Mollie turned the set off and stood hands on hips gazing down at Claire. "Not even a whisper," she said.

The werewolf groaned, and sat up. "I noticed." She held her left paw up, as if reluctant to place any weight on it. "There's a little metal tray on the desk. Pour another bottle of that caffeine into it. It's easier for me to lap up."

Mollie did so, setting the tray on the carpet. "I don't suppose you could use a straw."

"With these lips? Besides, if I'm going to be arrested, it will be for something a little more exciting than illegal possession of a banned object."

Mollie settled onto the desk chair. "That highway is traveled enough," she said, thinking her way. "Someone surely would have found the body by now."

Claire's voice was deathly quiet. "I know."

A dark cloud of fear and uncertainty swept through Mollie. "You know more than that."

"Yes."

"Claire—"

"But I'm not sure I know what I know."

"Oh, that makes about as much sense as giving you a straw."

The werewolf laughed. It sounded like the bark of a Pekinese.

"We're going to get thrown out of here," said Mollie.

Claire sat up again, this time able to place both front paws on the floor, if gingerly. "If you didn't know me, or know of me," she began, "you might explain the condition of that man's body by the attack of a wild animal. A wolf, or a bear, perhaps. There is no reason for the local authorities not to alert the local citizenry that such a creature might be lurking about. Think of the safety of the children, and so on."

She sighed, and took a moment to lick at the wound just back of her left shoulder.

"Which means," she finished, "someone knows, or at least strongly suspects."

Mollie scowled. "But...how?"

"I had my DNA tested, discreetly and quietly," Claire replied. "It is a blend of human and lupine elements. It is standard procedure these days for the coroner to test the DNA and run it against the registry. Mine will cause them some puzzlement. Either the man was attacked by a human or a wolf...or both."

Mollie's lips formed a silent, "Oh."

"It would be in the blood I left at the scene, and in...the saliva in the bites."

The werewolf yawned.

"Claire!" cried Mollie.

"It's all right. I'm okay."

"Don't scare me like that."

"I'm sorry." Claire got to her feet and came to lick Mollie's bare shin.

Mollie shivered. "Oh, and don't do that. It's..."

Claire sat back. "Arousing?" She laughed again.

"So what do we do?"

"We wait for me to recover and transform, and then we go directly to the bed."

"Claire," said Mollie, exasperated.

"I *am* serious. That's all we *can* do for now." The werewolf considered. "But I probably should let Travis know I'm around. He should already have sensed me, but we tend to be solitary creatures."

Mollie stood with fists on hips. "Oh, really."

"Do you see any other werewolves here?"

"Oh. Right."

Limping slightly on her left front paw, Claire began to

pace the room. "Of course, if I contact him, he'll know why. But that may be helpful; he'll also know I'm not his enemy."

Mollie flopped onto the bed. "I don't understand."

"We, ah, like each other."

"Oh!"

"It's not like that," Claire hastened to add. "Not anymore. It's the DNA again. Wolves mate for life. Humans, not so much. We hybrids tend to compromise." She paused, laughing. "This sounds like we're having a relationship discussion."

"It certainly does," Mollie said primly.

The werewolf padded over to her, and sat at her feet. Presently she licked at Mollie's knee. "I choose a life with you," she said solemnly.

Mollie bent and put her nose to Claire's. It was cold and wet. "Sorry. Sometimes I get insecure."

Claire hopped up on the bed. "Dial the phone," she said, and gave her the number.

Mollie did so. "Why do they still say 'dial,' I wonder. Nobody nowadays—"

"Hello?"

Mollie put the phone on speaker. "Travis?"

"So far, so good. I gather this is not a business call. My car's warranty is still good, and I already have cable, and I don't make time for a few questions regarding my voting habits."

Mollie set the phone down on the bed and stared at it.

"He's a character," whispered Claire.

The voice at the other end fell silent for so long that Mollie was afraid they'd been disconnected. There was the sound of a throat clearing. Then: "Claire." It was not a question.

"Hello, Trav. Long time."

"Yeah...wait! That's your...you know, voice."

"I have a problem," said Claire.

"You shouldn't have eaten the opossum."

"No, I...what?"

"Where are you?"

Claire told him.

"Who's the human?" he asked.

Mollie gaped at the phone. Her lips formed, "The human?"

"She knows, Travis."

"I'm glad you found someone. It'll be a few minutes. I'll knock."

The connection broke.

"The human?" Mollie said again, this time smiling. After a moment, she added, "How are you feeling?"

"Better." She curled her muzzle to lick at the left shoulder wound. "You can stop fretting. But I do still need to stay awake." Finished with her shoulder, Claire jumped down from the bed to land gingerly on the carpet. "See if you can find another news channel."

Mollie keyed the remote, flipped through several mainstream channels, and shook her head. "It's all national news now. We won't find anything local until nine or ten o'clock." She brightened. "I have a Kindle. You could read a book."

The werewolf paused, the hint of a smile on her mouth. "I prefer books with pages."

"Tough. Let me see. I have...ah, *White Fang*."

"Don't tease me."

Mollie got up to walk around. Her hands fluttered in frustration. "I hate not doing anything," she complained. "But I don't know what to do."

The werewolf padded alongside her. Every few seconds her muzzle nuzzled Mollie's thigh. "It's just for a little while longer," she soothed. "We'll resolve this matter with Travis, and then go out to the beach north of here. You'll like it."

"If we don't get caught."

Claire was silent.

"What?" said Mollie. She skidded to a stop on the carpet. "What aren't you telling me?"

"It's probably nothing."

"Claire..."

The werewolf sat down. "You know I have a past. It

could catch up with me someday." She raised her nose to sniff the air. "Someone just pulled into the lot."

Mollie gaped at her. "You can *smell* that?"

"No, I can hear that. I was trying to smell it. I've got nothing, yet."

Mollie went to the window and peered around the edge of the curtain. "They're parking right next to our car."

"Police?"

She shook her head. "I don't think so. One man, about our age. Casual dress. He's carrying a Palmetto." She reset the curtain and moved to the door. "You'd better stay in the bathroom."

Claire did not budge. "Describe him."

Mollie peeked again. "Tallish, medium brown hair, left-handed, erect—"

"How can you tell?"

Mollie gave an amused gasp. "He's carrying it in right hand, is how."

"Um...carrying what?"

"The Palmetto!"

"Oh! Right."

The expected knock came: two, then one, then two.

"Travis," said Claire. "Open it."

Mollie did so. The man with the Palmetto stood just outside the doorway. His grin of greeting failed when the open door revealed her.

"I'm sorry," he said, and started to turn. His nostrils worked, and he peered inside. "No, this is the right place."

Mollie stepped back. "Come in out of the sun," she invited.

Once inside, Travis only had eyes for Claire, sitting on the floor beside the bed. He stepped to her and sat down, his free hand coming to rest on her shoulder. Mollie gaped at her; her tail had begun to wag.

"Three years," he said, rubbing the werewolf's ears. "And I see you've been shot again."

"It was in a good cause."

"It always is, with you." He looked at Mollie, and explained. "She took a bullet for me, back when. Not as serious as these appear to be, though."

"She's healing," Mollie said stiffly, feeling a bit of green eye. "But she has to stay awake."

Travis paled a little. "Heart?"

Mollie nodded. Claire said, "Almost done. Another hour or so."

"Another...hour?"

Mollie's own heart began to pound, although she had no idea why. "What's wrong?" she demanded.

"Nothing," Travis said quickly. "Nothing's wrong." His gaze twitched, first to the window, then back at Mollie. "Why are you—"

Mollie pointed to the door. "Get out of here," she yelled. "Now!"

"Mollie!" cried Claire.

She threw the door open. "Something's wrong," she snapped at Claire. "I don't know, but...damn it, *go*!"

The sound of engines revved and tires skidding on gravel burst into the room.

"No!" screamed Mollie. "Claire, out the back window now. Go go go!"

She punctuated this by hurling the coffee maker at Travis, who did not duck quite in time. Hot coffee splashed over him, and he cried out in agony. The shimmering shape of a wolf started to come into focus, but he fought off the transformation. The back window shattered; Claire had escaped.

Two uniformed police officers dashed into the room, one with a pistol out, the other with a shotgun. Mollie froze. Wiping coffee from himself with the bed's comforter, Travis cursed her, and finally raised his hands. Two more officers, and a detective in plain clothes followed. Only the detective brandished no weapon.

"Is this her?" he asked Travis. All four officers aimed their weapons at Mollie, who blanched.

Travis shook his head. "But she's a witness, and she knows where the werewolf went."

"Where did it go?" asked the detective.

"Out the back window," Travis answered.

"I was asking her." He gave Mollie a hard look. "Well?"

"I don't know."

"She lies," said Travis.

"I certainly do not," snapped Mollie. "She did not tell me where she was going."

"They have a relationship," Travis told the detective. "They'll get together again."

The detective lifted a hand. "Wait. Wait a minute. Do you mean she and...and...that's *sick*."

"If you're not here to arrest me," said Mollie, "then you may all leave. *Now*."

The officers looked at one another. The detective said, "We can take you downtown for questioning, if that's the way you want it."

"Not until I talk with my lawyer."

"Who's that?" he asked.

"Whoever the court assigns at my arraignment."

Travis approached the detective, and they spoke so quietly that Mollie could not make out their words. Finally the detective said, "Very well. You've committed no crime." A whirl of his hand in the air bade the officers follow him out the door.

"You, too," Mollie said to Travis, venomously. "You traitor."

Travis spread his hands in a plea. "You don't understand..."

"Just tuck that yellow tail between your legs and get out."

Travis loped through the doorway. Mollie slammed the door behind him. "Now, what?" she sighed. "Claire, what am I supposed to do now?"

The question went unanswered. Only the echoes of the police intrusion and Travis's betrayal remained, the latter sickening Mollie. A few months ago she would have collapsed onto the carpet, helpless and inert. Since encountering Claire, however, one thought guided her, especially when times were difficult, as these were: *the kind of girl she wants*. So what would that girl do now?

Mollie did not trust Travis even an iota. Something was up with him.

Okay: what?

Well...unless the police and Travis could find Claire on their own, the only connection they had was her, Mollie. Surely, with the werewolf psychic connection, Travis could locate Claire, just as he had to have located her here at the motel. Therefore...

Mollie's heart sank. Therefore, either Claire was unconscious or worse, or she was able to block probes from Travis.

Mollie bolted to the rear window, through which Claire had escaped. A stretch of unmown grass led to a mixed forest fifty yards away. The trees had grown so densely that little sunlight penetrated. She doubted she could locate Claire within, assuming the werewolf was there at all. Worse, in an hour or so, it would be dark.

That left option number two: the police assumed she knew where Claire had gone; so did Travis. In the forest, mommy bird leads the snake *away* from the nest.

She wondered how much there was in the Denali's gas tank.

A wicked grin slashed her face: *Let's find out.*

The last of the rush hour traffic clotted Highway 101. Mollie had seen worse, but had not driven in it. She kept one eye on the rearview and the other on the left side mirror, checking for tails and for a spot where she could merge into the stream of cars. Two vehicles had followed her up the ramp: a brown sedan that might be a Dodge, and a silver-gray Nissan. Either or neither or both might be following her. With no experience at detecting a tail, she could only hope to spot a vehicle whose actions matched hers. As soon as she reached the highway, she kept the Denali to the right lane, slowing for merging vehicles that were more like barging vehicles.

Emergency lights ahead alerted her to a vehicle on the right shoulder, and she slowed, following the law. This brought the vehicle behind her—a sporty red pickup—to within a couple feet of her rear bumper. Apparently safe driving was a no-no in Oregon. She muttered disgustedly and accelerated back to sixty-five. The pickup remained on her bumper for another hundred yards or so, then swung into the left lane to pass, honking as it drove by.

"Good luck with that bridge abutment," she said, mostly to herself.

Both the Dodge and the Nissan remained behind her, three and four cars back, respectively. At the junction with Sixth Street, the Nissan turned off toward the ocean. That left the brown Dodge. Presently she came upon Second Street, and took it, heading west and then northwest. The Dodge stayed with her, four cars back now. She stopped at a light and took stock.

If she attempted to lose the tail, it would signal to the driver of the Dodge that she had tumbled to the surveillance. To lose it, then, she would have to do it seemingly inadvertently. In a city filled with stop lights and stop signs, quickness of decision and action would do her no good. She would have to be sneaky.

The light changed. Ahead on the left was a fast-food burger joint. She made the turn, the Dodge following after a couple on-coming vehicles cleared. Mollie swung the Denali around to the rear, where there was a line for the drive-through. She pulled into a slot along the curb, turned off the engine, and got out, making sure to lock the doors. The Dodge was nowhere in sight.

Mollie entered the joint through the door on that side and got in line. Presently a middle-aged man with short salt-and-pepper hair came in through the other side door and stood back, as if assessing the menu on the wall above the serving counter. Mollie ignored him. When her turn came, she ordered a burger meal to eat in, and paid for it. When she asked about the rest room, the clerk pointed her in the right direction.

As she had noticed beforehand, the trip to the rest room took her around to a passageway that paralleled the side on which she had parked. When she reached the door to the ladies' room, she pushed it open, but did not enter. Instead, she allowed the door to close again. The sounds it made were just loud enough to be heard in the lobby. She then left the joint through another side door, one that could not be seen from the lobby.

Key already in her hand, Mollie swiftly reached the Denali, climbed in, started it up, backed out, and took off. She dared not look too long at the lobby, but she did catch a glimpse of the man moving into position where he could observe the passageway to the rest rooms. She made two turns, running a stop sign at the second one, and made the highway again, this time heading back north, toward the motel.

She kept the Denali at just over the speed limit, even though that meant she would be passed by most other vehicles on the highway. But there was method to her behavior: most vehicles *would* pass—but it seemed unlikely that anyone tailing her would do so, unless they were part of a team. The rearview and side mirrors were her guides, and she kept a close eye on them as she drove. She had no intention of returning to the motel. They would expect that, and Claire would know that. She would also expect Mollie to know.

"Girl she wants," muttered Mollie, smiling.

The next motel was on the sea side of the highway. Mollie drove to the next turn, crossed over, and head back toward it. The *Utter Limits* consisted of an office that trailed units, the way a train engine trails boxcars. Of the five cars parked there, none came within five years of the Denali. An inexpensive, out-of-the-way place, then.

Of course, she thought wryly, Claire could have headed south. Mollie parked near the office entrance and remained in the vehicle, considering. After a moment, she gave herself a tiny shake of the head. No, Claire would not head south, for that's where the people were. She needed privacy and anonymity for her recovery. Mollie's heart and chest ached. How was Claire doing? *Do I need to be proactive and go find her, or will she find me? Will she even know where to look?*

Mollie went inside the office to register. Either the A/C

was off, or there was none. The clerk was easily in his fifties, recently shaved but not today, with sparse graying hair and rheumy blue eyes. The top of his head might come to her chin. Unimpressed, Mollie veiled her opinion behind a pleasant smile.

"I'd like a room, please."

The man grunted, and slid a registration form across the counter to her. She filled it out, indicating an occupancy for one, and non-smoking. Vaguely she wondered why that last was even an option. She also took out her driver's license and laid it on the counter. He picked it up with fingers yellowed by tobacco and examined it as if it were somehow contaminated. Finally he jotted some numbers on the registration form, and told her the amount. She passed him a Visa, he slotted it, waited for the receipt, and had her sign it, before giving her a key card. She was tempted to count her fingers before she left.

Mollie had landed Unit #13, the one at the far end of the train. Units 8 through 12 were empty; at least, there were no vehicles parked in front of them. The parking spot in front of her door had a water-filled pothole that she narrowly avoided by taking the spot for Unit 12. With the motor still running, she looked from right to left and back again, and over her shoulder. Nobody seemed interested in anything she might be doing—but that didn't mean they weren't watching.

Her hands shook as she shut off the motor and climbed out of the Denali. Give them something to do, she told herself. Slot the key card before someone sees you. The door snicked open. Quickly she stepped inside and shut the door, locking the knob and sliding the deadbolt. She paused with her back to it, gasping for breath.

The room was hot, the heavy blue curtains drawn over the front window. She hit the light switch, and was pleasantly surprised to find that it worked. In the dim light she saw that the bed was a single, and had been made, with an extra pillow thrown in in case she wanted to sit up and read. There was a nightstand and a desk, the lamp and wooden chair its accouterments. A rickety dresser invited her clothing.

She checked the bathroom. It seemed clean enough. No hair in the sink or in the shower drain. Typical coarse white towels, two bars—if one could call them that—of complimentary floral-scented soap, a mat to stand on while she dried. A few stains on the linoleum around the base of the toilet bowl. She looked out the back window and saw a ribbon of sparsely-grassed sand that gave onto a low ridge and then the beach. She was about fifty yards from the ridge and maybe fifteen feet above the waves that came to die a frothy death on the sand.

You're in a mood, she told herself.

On impulse she opened the window and climbed out—she was just slender enough to accomplish this. To the south along the shore, two or three people were shuffling along, apparently looking for shells or other objects of interest. To the north, a rocky wall jutted out into the ocean, occupied by sea birds, although she thought she heard the barks of a sea lion.

The bathroom window to Unit #12 was also open. This disconcerted her. She had not realized she'd parked in a slot that belonged to another occupant. She leaned in and started to call out.

"Woof!" said Claire, popping up, and Mollie passed out.

003: On the Run

Mollie awoke to a cold washcloth laid across her forehead. Beyond that broke Claire's smile at seeing her eyes open. The room was dark, the lights off. Claire smelled of cinnamon; the room smelled of smoke and sweat, both old. Mollie sat up, felt dizzy, and fell back.

"What timezit?" she mumbled.

Claire sat down on the edge of the bed. "Just after sunset. The Pacific horizon is a sailor's delight. Pinks and salmons to lavenders and purples. Stars like a donut topped with sprinkles. Or glitter."

Mollie grinned up at her. "Waxing poetic, are we?"

"I'm back to my normal hairy self, and you're with me. Travis won't be on television until tomorrow night. We have time to locate him, and..."

"And?" pressed Mollie.

"I don't know. I really don't know. But we have to protect ourselves. That includes you, by the way."

That surprised Mollie. "You mean other werewolves would protect me?"

"No, probably not. But they know *I* would protect you. I ordered pizza, it should be here in about ten minutes."

"Veggie, of course."

"Your half is sausage." Claire stood up. "Better get dressed. We don't want to shock the delivery person."

"I'm naked," said Mollie, with belated realization.

"When someone faints, you're supposed to loosen the clothing," Claire said sagely. "It facilitates the respiration."

"Any port in a storm."

Claire rapped a knuckle on Mollie's kneecap. "Something like that. C'mon, up you go."

* * *

The meal arrived without incident. Claire had paid for it with a credit card in another name, so that government surveillance would take scant notice of it. There was, of course, always the chance that credit card sales for delivered meals in the Florence area currently received emphatic focus. Even so, the odds were slim that the NSA or any other acronym would tumble to the purchase of pizzas by one Jerrold Parsons. The young man who delivered the pizzas clearly assumed, by the expression on his face, that Parsons, who supposedly was in the shower, had also recruited some local talent to keep his bed warm. That, too, was as Claire had expected.

The delivery included a six-pack of sodas, and Mollie found that she was more thirsty than hungry. She downed the last of the third sausage slice with a "now what?" look on her face.

"I have to be closer to sense him," said Claire. "I have his address. I thought we'd try that tonight. But he may already be under police protection."

"So how do we—?"

"I'll think of something."

"That's what scares me," said Mollie.

The last slice of veggie pizza awaited attention. They both grabbed for it, and Mollie won. Claire took the remains of the mozzarella in the box.

"We'll use this," said Claire, hefting the closed box. "It's a perfect ruse. You'll deliver."

Mollie frowned hard. "Won't they be watching?"

Claire shook her head. "You, *p'tite*. They'll be watching you. I'll be climbing through the back window. By the time Travis figures it out, I'll be on him."

Mollie mulled this. "But what if he changes?"

"He can't do that if he's unconscious."

"It's almost two hours until dark."

Claire smiled. "I think we can find something to do until then."

* * *

Darkness cloaked them. From behind the bank of lilacs across the street they observed the house. It was a simple affair, designed by a cookie-cutter architect for the housing project. If it had more than one bedroom, Mollie would have been surprised. Although the curtains were drawn over the front windows, shadows moved within. Claire was unable to determine whether a shadow was Travis; to do so, to sense him, she would have to open herself to detection as well. She made a face and shook her head at Mollie, the movement shaking a few thin branches.

"What about that car parked down the street?" asked Mollie. "Can you use your spidey-sense to see if anyone is in it? Like a cop, maybe?"

Again Claire shook her head. "But it is parked facing the wrong direction," she pointed out. "I think we have to chance it." She rose carefully. "Give me three minutes to get into position."

"Wait. How do I explain the fact that I have no car outside?"

"You won't have to. By the time he opens the door, I'll be inside and right behind him."

Mollie pursed her lips in protest, but said nothing. If she were certain of but one thing on this planet, it was that Claire would protect her. But could she protect her in time?

She counted to sixty, and another sixty. Claire had already made it to the side of the house and had vanished into the foliage. Mollie felt the urge to call out, "Ready or not, here I come." The thought lightened her mood and dampened her doubts. She was certain that another sixty seconds had passed. She reviewed the plan. Cross the street, ring the doorbell and add a couple raps on the door for good measure, and wait, trying to hold onto the pizza box with fingers crossed. Simple. Travis would recognize her immediately after opening the door. Timing was critical. Claire had to slug him before he could transform. Otherwise...

But she tried not to think about that as she dashed across the street in the dim light. With the pizza box held flat, as if to protect the contents, she made her way up the sidewalk, up the step, and to the door. Rang the bell, added a knock. Waited. All according to plan.

Nothing.

Not a sound...

No, a gong, and then a thump, like a body falling.

The door opened, and Mollie yelped. She stumbled backwards, and almost off the porch. Claire caught her, and tugged her inside.

Mollie dropped the pizza box and pressed her hand over her heart. Her respiration was rapid and shallow. "Don't ever," she gasped, but was unable to finish. Questions filled her eyes.

"He just sat there," explained Claire, her eyes filled with disbelief. "A ring and a knock and he just sat there. He didn't even blink."

"He's on something," was Mollie's assessment. She paused at the dinette and gazed at the body slumped on the floor next to the table. "What did you do to him?"

Claire pointed to an aluminum cooking pot with a dent in the bottom of it. "I can't believe I was able to get that close to him," she said. "You may be right." She sniffed the air. "But it's not pot."

"Fentanyl?" tried Mollie.

"Could be." She looked around. "That, or some other opioid. Whatever it is, it's probably still here. I wonder..."

"Call the police, tell them you tried to deliver a pizza, but the guy was just too violent and making crazy noises, and you ran off?"

Claire clapped her on the back. "Now you're thinking like a werewolf. I'll make the call. Let's go further down the street and watch what happens."

Less than five minutes later, the police arrived: two cars with blue lights flashing, but no sirens. Four officers emerged, two with weapons drawn. Claire had left the door slightly ajar, an open invitation for the police to enter. There were shots, and a crash that was audible and reached the Denali, a block away. A large wolf fled toward the woods. It was impossible to determine whether he had been wounded.

"Suddenly I don't feel good about this," said Claire.

"What's on the other side of that woods?"

Claire frowned. "More woods. Oh, and a road that

connects two outlying areas. Turn around. Maybe we can catch up to him."

"And do what?" said Mollie, putting the SUV in gear.

"First things first. Drive!"

GPS was useless; Mollie had no idea where they were headed. On impulse Claire had her turn left, then right, and an immediate second left. This road had a rural appearance: two lanes, no center stripes, thick forest on the left. The Denali's headlights dissipated in the distance. Driving too fast for them, Mollie turned on the high beams. It gave her a better view of the road's shoulders.

"Deer," said Claire.

Mollie blinked, and peered into the darkness. "I don't see—" she began, and emitted a soft squeal as a deer emerged from the trees a hundred feet ahead and stopped in the middle of the road. Its eyes glowed back at them as Mollie applied the brakes hard. "Spidey-sense works just fine, I see," she said.

Claire did not respond. Mollie glanced at her, and saw that she was transforming.

"Travis?" she said, unnecessarily.

"It won't help all that much," said Claire. "But keep the doors locked and the windows rolled up anyway."

"We're stopped in the middle of the road at night," worried Mollie. "What-what are you going to do?"

"Wait. Watch. You can pull us over to the shoulder," she added as an after-thought.

Mollie did so. Almost immediately the werewolf beside her opened the passenger door and slipped out into the night. Mollie shivered. Even as she watched, a werewolf fairly flew from the forest and landed on the deer, slamming it to the ground. A single bite to its throat raised a fountain of blood. The deer's legs kicked violently. But the werewolf seemed to pause in its butchery. It shook itself. In the headlights, Mollie could see it had to be Travis. So where was Claire?

The werewolf that was Travis slowly slumped on top of the deer. But not to feed. He simply did not move from that point. In that moment, Claire came into view. She sniffed at Travis, and looked as if she wanted to howl. But she kept her composure, and clomping her jaws on his ankle, dragged him onto the shoulder and beyond, into the bushes. Already Mollie could see that he was transforming back into his human self.

The headlights failed to locate either of them. Mollie's ribs ached, and she realized she had been holding her breath. A huge inhalation failed to calm her, or slow her heart rate. What had just happened? Where was Claire? It seemed to her that some shrubbery branches were moving. It might have been her imagination, or the wind, or a trick of the night. Why did werewolves have to do their rough stuff in the dark?

The handle of the passenger door rattled, and Mollie screamed. Claire was at the window, transformed back to herself. Mollie unlocked the door for her.

"What," she asked, "happened?"

Claire stared out into the night. Mollie knew better than to break into her thoughts, but she knew something bad had transpired. The deer on the roadway kicked its last, and lay still.

"He's dead," said Claire, her voice as soft as starlight.

"What...*how*?"

Claire shook her head. "Drive," she said. "Drive on. We have to get out of here."

Mollie pulled around the deer carcass, while Claire dug the map from the glove box and examined it in the overhead light. The light interfered with Mollie's vision, and she had to squint through the window shield to see clearly.

"Sorry," murmured Claire. Presently she shut out the light and replaced the map. "It looks like this road takes us to Brickerville," she said, getting out her Palmetto. "From there, we can get back on 126 and go to Eugene. Meanwhile, I have to make a phone call."

"Claire, what happened to Travis?"

"I think he OD'ed on something," she replied, uncertainty in her tone. "Oxycodone, maybe. It put too great a strain on his heart, along with the transformation and the activity of running. Being a werewolf wouldn't help him there."

"But...his body..."

"I dragged it further into the woods. It will be found eventually, but by then we'll be long gone."

Mollie's brow knit. "But...but I was followed in Florence," she said. "I lost them, but if they got the license plate."

"Not to worry."

"But—"

"If they trace it at all, they'll find that Belinda Miner, who looks remarkably like me, rented the Denali," Claire explained. "Miner, a resident of Fargo, North Dakota, returned the keys at night through the slot." She punctuated this with a shrug.

"So no trace."

"Fingerprints, maybe. Mine aren't on file anywhere."

"Brickerville, four miles."

"So I see."

Mollie fretted. "But my fingerprints are in the car."

"They aren't on file, right? And even if they are, and someone asks you, you can always say you hitched a ride, and while Belinda was off shopping or whatever, she let you use the car until she called you."

"But...how did I get back to Arizona?"

"Who said we're going back to Arizona?"

"Claire..."

Claire held up a hand for silence as she tokked a number on the Palmetto, and put it on speaker. After the third ring, a male voice said, "Go."

"Travis Becker is down for the count," said Claire. "Suspected OD. He was human when he died." She added his location, and finished, "We're on our way out of here. So far, so good."

"I'm sorry," said the voice. "But."

"Yeah," said Claire. "But. I'm out," she said, and closed the Palmetto.

"Claire, you're scaring me," said Mollie. Her voice

broke. "Is there...is there, like, a werewolf Underground or something? It sure sounds like there is."

"There is," Claire told her. "I shouldn't have to explain to you what would happen in this country, or all over the world, if it should be discovered that we are real. You think the Salem witch trials were bad? And you know how easily people are stampeded by fear, and by the media. A lot of innocent people would be killed."

"I know, I know." Gently but firmly Mollie pounded the steering wheel with the flat of her right hand. "But...did we come here to...to..."

"To kill Travis? No, just to talk him out of exposing himself and us. But it didn't work out that way."

She glanced at Claire, as much for reassurance as to see whether she was telling the truth. "You promise?"

"Mollie..." She sounded as if she wanted to cry. "I don't wish anyone dead. None of us do. It's just that... sometimes things happen. It's a process, coming to terms with who you are. I'm at peace with myself. I control my changes. Not all of us have learned to do that. But the me you know, is me. That, I promise you."

"I didn't mean to upset you."

For a couple minutes Mollie silently digested all this. Having never been associated with a death before, she struggled with her feelings regarding the tragedy. But the overarching theme was Claire's love. The werewolf had pulled Mollie's life out of the doldrums and given it purpose and happiness. It was just that...that...

Mollie shook her head to clear it. Claire said, "Turn right up here. That'll get us back to 126."

"I need a shower and a bed." With a glance at Clair, Mollie added, "A big bed."

"Maybe we should drop off this car and go to a different rental and get another."

Mollie made the turn. "What good would that do?"

"We'll just go. East, I think, as west eventually is apt to be a bit damp."

Mollie barked laughter.

"And you can sleep while I drive," added Claire.

After a change of vehicles in Eugene, they took Interstate 5 to Corvallis, then U.S. 20 southeast toward Burns, heading ultimately for the Idaho border and Interstate 84. By the time they reached Burns over four hours later, it was well past midnight, and Mollie had climbed into the back seat and gone to sleep. Claire, whose night vision and alertness was excellent, drove on. With the radio off, she hummed a few tunes, tapping out a rhythm on the steering wheel of the Dodge Journey. At one point she was about to howl, and held back at the last second, lest she alarm Mollie.

In the silence and solitude of the front seat, with her senses on full, she allowed her thoughts to drift to Mollie, sprawled along the back seat with a folded jacket for a pillow. Fortune had favored Claire. So few women were open to the idea of a relationship with a werewolf. They failed to realize that a werewolf was merely a human with the capacity to change. Just like most other humans. Education, experience, weather, employment, all induced changes in people. Some grew fat, others grew thin, and some changed into wolves on occasion. Viewed from that perspective, werewolves were not all that unusual, their tendency toward eating venison raw notwithstanding.

Claire, of course, being vegetarian in her human aspect, carried that over into her werewolf self as well. Being a werewolf didn't change who you really were, inside, where it counted most. She reached into a ziplock bag and pulled out a little stalk of celery, and began to munch as she drove.

Traffic was almost non-existent at this time of night. A semi or two, a stray car, that was all they had encountered since passing by Juntura. But now, as they reached the winding part of the highway, a pair of headlights behind her appeared and gradually closed. She checked the speedometer and slowed to the limit of fifty-five. The spacing of the headlights suggested a smaller vehicle...but the police were known to employ such cars nowadays, as they were cheaper and easier on gas, if virtually useless in setting up roadblocks.

The vehicle continued to close. Claire estimated its speed at around seventy—too fast for a winding highway at night. She decided to slow a little more to encourage the car to pass her. As expected, it veered into the other lane—without using the turn signal, she noted—and swept on by. It cut back in front of her barely two car-lengths ahead, seemed to fishtail for a second, and sped on. Claire, who had slowed even more as the car almost cut her off, resumed her normal speed, while the vehicle ahead disappeared over a rise and around a bend and down into the next valley.

Someone, she thought, in a hurry. She hoped the driver knew the road, even in the dark. The Malheur River off to the left made the bends even more precarious. Still, she did not allow herself to be overly concerned. People often drove as if they were immortal, or at least invulnerable. She, whose lupine blood and DNA would enable her to live longer than three human lifetimes, had few worries on that score. She drove safely so as not to attract attention, and on this occasion so as not to dislodge Mollie. And because she simply enjoyed driving.

Cresting the rise, she saw in the distance headlights pointing straight up. Snarling a curse, she accelerated to the limits of safety. As she drew closer, she saw that the vehicle had missed a curve and wound up trunk-down against the steep side of a cut draw. She parked well off the shoulder, glanced back to see that Mollie was all right, and got out of the Dodge.

The hood of the vehicle—she saw now that it was a dark Honda sedan—had crumped against the rocks as the car had made a valiant effort to climb the slope. The driver's side door had sprung, slightly ajar now but bent so that it would not open. Through the broken window Claire could see a motionless figure. A quick sniff identified it as a male. Another sniff detected gasoline.

Claire drew up by the vehicle and tugged at the door. It refused to budge. Now she had no choice. The transformation burst her jeans, so that they fell in a heap around her feet. It also shredded her cropped top. Fully werewolf now, she freed the rags from her body and reached again for the door. Forced by superhuman strength, it gave readily enough, but as it did, the driver spilled down from the seat. She caught both him and door in her front paws, and shoved the door aside. And stared.

The driver was a boy about twelve or thirteen years old. W, she thought, TF.

His eyelids fluttered. He opened them. And screamed.

The scream echoed along the river. Crying out now, eyes huge, he tried without success to kick at Claire. She set him down gently on the grass and gravel, and held him down with her paw on his chest. In the deep guttural voice of the werewolf she said, "I won't hurt you."

The words shocked him, more by the fact of them than by their meaning.

"What happened?" called Mollie, climbing out of the Dodge Journey.

Claire turned around. Already she was beginning to transform back to human. "Hold him here," she said.

While Mollie did so, Claire completed her transformation. She was dressed only in briefs and the remnants of the cropped top. The smell of wet dog joined that of the gasoline.

Mollie knelt down beside the boy. "Are you all right?" she asked.

"She's a werewolf!" he cried, and resumed his struggles.

"Yeah, I know. It's a neat trick at parties." She shook him for emphasis. "Are you all right? What hurts?"

"Are you...are you a..."

"No, I'm not," Mollie replied, smiling. "Please. You are in no danger. We're only trying to help."

Claire sniffed the air again. "I don't smell blood from him," she said. "But that gas is getting worse. Let's get him into the car."

"Are you all right?" Mollie asked him again.

"Yeah. Yeah...I think so. My head hurts."

She checked him for injuries, and found a couple of small lumps on his skull. Neither was bleeding. She got him to his feet, and steadied him as they walked to the Journey, with Claire trailing. A couple times he tried to pull back when he noticed Claire, and Mollie reassured him as best she could. When they reached the SUV, she opened the back door for him.

He peered inside as if something might be lurking there. "It's all right," Mollie told him. "Nothing is going to hurt you."

He glanced over his shoulder. "She could."

"Not while she's driving."

His eyes widened. "She's *driving*?"

Mollie dropped to one knee. "Look, I know this is hard for you to understand," she said, gently but firmly. "Yes, my friend is a werewolf. But she is nothing like you see in the movies or on television."

"She-she doesn't eat people?"

"She eats tofu, right out of the box."

"Eww."

Mollie laughed, as did Claire. "She's a vegetarian," Mollie told him. "She won't even bite her fingernails. Now please, get in. Then we'll talk, so we can figure out a way to help you. Oh, and I'm Mollie, and she's Claire. What's your name?"

"It's Paulie. Paulie Rummell."

"I'm pleased to meet you, Paul," said Mollie, deliberately giving him the name of an older boy, and shook his hand. She climbed into the back seat beside him. Claire held out her hand to him, but he pulled back, wide eyes staring at it as if it were still a paw.

"It's all right, Paul," she said. "I understand." She peered into the dark along the highway. "We'd better get out of here before someone comes along."

Silence followed as they continued down the highway. After they passed Harper without seeing a single vehicle, Claire nodded to herself. "So far, so good," she said.

Mollie put her arm around the boy. "Talk to us," she urged him. "Tell us what the problem is. Maybe we can fix it."

Paul's lips worked as if he were trying to form the right words.

"Did you run away from home?" Mollie asked him.

"How-how did you know...?"

"I ran away from home, too," Claire said. "When I was not much older than you. It wasn't a lot of fun."

"Were you...you know...?"

"A werewolf?" Claire chuckled. "No, that came later. No, I ran away because my stepfather drank too much, and when he drank..."

"Yeah," said Paul. "I know."

"So where were you going?" asked Mollie.

In the dark of the back seat, his face lit up. "My Mom's in Twin Falls."

"Wow," said Claire. "You were driving all the way there? Where did you come from?"

"Do you know where Hines is?"

Mollie nodded. "I think we passed it about two hours ago. You must really have wanted to get away, Paul."

"It's...it's Paulie."

"Anyone who's old enough to drive that far in the dark deserves to be called a man's name," said Claire. "With us, you're Paul."

"O-okay."

"Whose car was that?" Mollie asked him.

"M-my stepdad's."

"Good one," said Claire. She reached into the back seat. "Slap me five."

To her surprise, after a very brief hesitation, Paul did. He punctuated the slap with a laugh, and Claire felt the ice starting to melt.

"So what we have to do," said Mollie, "is get you to your mother's place."

"It's probably a little more complicated than that," Claire said. "Custody, weekends, alimony, child support. We don't know what the agreements were. And I hate to say it, but we don't know anything about..."

"Yeah," said Mollie, in synch with her. "Except for one

telling fact: he wants to go there."

"There is that," agreed Claire. "We're coming up on Vale. Another twenty minutes or so, and we'll be on Interstate 84. Then it's Boise, and about two hours after that we'll be in Twin Falls."

"Are you going to drive all night?" asked Paul.

Claire grinned at him in the mirror. "I'm used to staying up all night."

To her surprise, he laughed. She thought that was a good sign.

"About Claire," said Mollie, struggling to find the right words.

"I won't tell anyone," Paul promised. "Not even my mother."

"Are you hungry?" she asked. "We can stop along the way for a bite to eat, if you like."

"You probably shouldn't have said 'bite'," Claire pointed out.

Paul laughed at that as well. "Yes, please," he said.

Mollie pulled him closer, so that he leaned on her. "Get some sleep if you can," she soothed. "We'll stop in Boise, about an hour from now. I'll be right here."

"O-okay."

In the rearview, Claire smiled.

The bright lights of late-night Boise awoke Paul. For a moment he struggled, but Mollie soon hushed him. Blinking, he seemed to get his bearings. Claire took an exit and soon had them at the ordering window of a fast-food drive thru. Mollie and Paul ordered burgers and fries, while Claire settled for a tofu-burger. They parked near the back of the lot to eat.

The boy was suddenly ravenous. He continued to stuff his mouth until admonished by Mollie to slow down, that the food wasn't trying to escape. He temporized with a shot of soda through a straw.

"When did you eat last?" Claire asked him.

"I-I don't know. I guess...last night."

A police car drove in a circuit around the restaurant.

He passed their Dodge Journey with barely a glance, and drove out and onto the street. Mollie breathed a little sigh of relief.

"What would have happened if...?" Paul asked timidly. Clearly he was concerned that Claire might transform.

"We'd cooperate, as far as we could," Claire answered. "We try to avoid trouble; we don't go looking for it. I have a valid license, and so does Mollie. This is a rental car, and the papers are in order. You needn't worry about us."

"Maybe he was looking for me," he pointed out.

Claire met Mollie's eyes in the mirror. "That's something we hadn't considered," she said.

"But the police wouldn't know to look for this vehicle," Mollie argued.

"Oregon plates," Claire shot back. "They're probably fairly common here in Boise, but they'll narrow the search parameters." She took a noisy final sip of her chocolate shake. "We should move on."

She pulled the Journey onto the street and drove toward the on-ramp to get back onto Interstate 84. As she made the turn, a police car shot past on the street, heading in the direction of the restaurant they had just left. Claire issued a few words that widened Paul's eyes, but did not succumb to the urge to speed up the ramp any more than usual.

"Don't look back," she told them. "I'll keep watch in the rearview. I don't see anything."

Paul's voice, already pitched high, now quivered. "What's going to happen?"

"I don't know," Claire told him. "But we'll deal with it."

Mollie pulled him a little closer. "Hush and don't worry," she said. "We've got this. In another two hours or so, you'll be with your mother. Um...you *do* have her address, right?"

Again Claire swore. "I must be slipping. I never thought to ask."

"Yeah, I have it. I have an envelope in my back pocket." To verify this, he reached for it, and tugged it free. "See?"

"Don't lose it," admonished Mollie. "Put it back, and go to sleep. I'll wake you when we get to Twin Falls. Claire?"

"Still nothing."

Claire settled into the seat, and took the Journey up to seventy-five, which meant only half the vehicles on the road would pass her. After a glance back to check on Paul—his eyes were already closed—she transformed only slightly, giving herself a werewolf's night vision and more sensitive hearing. The transformations were sensory, not physical—something she had been practicing of late. It remained to be discovered how much of her she could accessorize—as she thought of it—without revealing her alter ego.

Exit signs whizzed past on the right, semis roared by on the left as they built up some speed prior to reaching the mountains. Claire drove steadily, with periodic rearview checks, but the only lights flashing belonged to the trucks as they signaled hello to one another.

Now a car came up in the left-hand lane, slowly passing the other vehicles. It was a good mile away when Claire spotted it. At first she assumed the driver was one of those idiots who had set his cruise control at seventy point three so that he could take six weeks passing vehicles going seventy point two. But something about the lights and the car's progress struck her as more deliberate than that. It looked to her as if someone in the vehicle was...looking for something...or someone.

Still, the police weren't about to search every vehicle with Oregon plates. For a moment that thought reassured her. But she remembered that some states required rentals to have codes on their plates. The police, then, might be looking for rentals, of which there would be far fewer.

Quietly she roused Mollie, and without awakening Paul, briefed her on what might be happening. After she had finished, Mollie asked, "So what can we do?"

"I don't know. He's still over half a mile back. If he pulls us over and realizes he has the vehicle they want, he won't do anything until help arrives. He'll just keep us here. One cop, I can deal with. If I'm shot, I can recover. But if it's four, five cops...and you know how cops are: they'd never fire two shots where forty would do, even if two-thirds of them missed. By the time I recovered..." She shook her head, and banged her flat hand a couple times on the steering wheel.

"What about a rest stop?"

"First place they'd look. And there isn't one for another...ten miles. Worse, there aren't any useful exits. We're in a military reservation and there's an air base south of us." Resignation crept into her tone. "Mollie, there's nowhere to go. If we could make the Gooding exit, we can take US 26 east and then State 75 south to Twin Falls. But that exit is a good eight miles past the rest stop...oh, crap. He's got his whirly lights on."

With no choice now, she gradually slowed the Journey, as other drivers were doing and poised to stop if necessary. The onrushing police vehicle was not slowing. It shot past them at a hundred or more and eventually disappeared into the night.

"Breathe," said Claire, pulling the Dodge back onto the pavement. "Your heart rate is over eighty. Slow, deep breaths, and hold each one a beat or two before you exhale."

"You...you can hear my heart?"

"There. It's starting to slow. Mollie, I...only transformed a little bit, to augment the senses. That's all."

"So you can see better at night."

"That's part of it, yeah. And the hearing. It's something I've been working on."

"You should have told me," groused Mollie.

"Yes, I should have." She glanced in the rearview, and met Mollie's eyes. "I should have done, *p'tite*. Forgive me."

"You know I do..."

The Journey slowed again. "Claire?" worried Mollie.

"Roadblock," she said, dejected. "About two miles ahead." She sighed. "We'll have to stop; no choice. Better wake Paul, and let him know what's going on."

The boy was cross at first. He squirmed away from Mollie; she let him go. While he glared at her in the dark, she explained what lay ahead. He peered between the front seats and into the darkness, and saw the lights and cars ahead.

"What's going to happen?" he fretted.

"I don't know yet," answered Claire. "Paul, you're Mollie's son. You're Paul Palmer. That's all you need to say, and only if you're asked. You're eleven—"

"Thirteen!" he protested.

"Tonight, you're eleven. Mollie, you can work out the math, right?"

"Understood."

"All right, then. Five more cars...now four."

The Interstate was full of flashing blue and red lights, and flashlights, and uniformed police officers. In addition, Claire spotted several men, some in suits, gathered at the perimeter of the roadblock. She doubted anyone in the other vehicles noticed them...or smelled their offices on them. She frowned at herself in the mirror; the roadblock seemed much larger than necessary to detain a boy in a stolen car.

Two cars...then one. Claire held her breath. A glance in the rearview at the back seat told her that Mollie was on edge.

"I love you," whispered Claire. "I will protect you."

Mollie seemed to relax; Paul had heard the sounds, but not the words. He scooted across the seat and back to Mollie.

Two police officers bracketed the Dodge Journey. One shined his flashlight into Claire's eyes, but she already had them narrowed in anticipation. The light moved to the back seat.

"License and registration, please," he said. It was not a question.

"I have to reach into my pocket for the license, officer," said Claire. "And into the glove box for the registration. This is a rental, and the agreement is there as well."

He kept his light on her hands. "Go ahead."

She managed to fumble the wallet out without unhooking the seat belt, and retrieved the paperwork. "There you go, officer."

He shined the light on her, and then on the license. "Claire De Lune?"

"As you see."

He gave the paperwork only a casual glance, and shined the light into the back seat. "Your name, Miss?"

"Mollie Palmer."

"And he is?"

"My son, Paul."

"How old are you, Paul?" asked the officer.

"E-eleven, s-sir."

The light went back to Mollie. "You must have had him when you were young."

"Hey, *I* made the mistake," Mollie snapped. "*He's* not a mistake. He's my son. Jeez, you people never let up, do you?"

He returned to Claire. "Have you picked up any hitchhikers along the way?"

"I'm not stupid, officer."

"Well, don't. There are two escapees from the Air Force stockade. They're armed and dangerous." He did not elaborate, but returned her license and paperwork. After one more flash of his light into the back seat, he waved them on.

No one spoke for two miles. Finally Mollie said, "Wow."

"Yeah. Paul, you did well back there, acting scared and nervous like that."

"I wasn't...wasn't acting."

"I was," said Mollie.

"Relax, you two. Another hour, Paul, and you'll be home."

He snuggled against Mollie again, and closed his eyes.

* * *

From twenty miles out, and even at four in the morning, Claire could see the glow of the city. It grew brighter as she approached. When the exits advisory came up, she gave the address for Paul's mother to the GPS and followed its instructions. Traffic lights now slowed her progress, and it was not until five o'clock that she reached the residential area. Driving the dark streets posed no problem, for she transformed her eyes a little more, until they could easily make out the address numbers. All the houses seemed to have been designed by the same architect—bungalows of a type, with the garage attached to the right side of the house, the front door offset to the left front, and a tree in the middle of the front yard. Paul's mother had a maple.

The house also had an empty driveway, and Claire pulled the Journey into it and shut off the lights and the engine. The lack of sound awoke Mollie.

"Are we there yet?" she asked, her grin glowing in the dark.

"The front door is ajar," Claire said softly. "If he awakens, keep him quiet. I'll go check."

"Claire..."

"I'll be careful, and I won't change unless I have to."

Carefully and quietly she got out of the SUV and crept to the door in the dark. Sniffing the air, she knew already what she was about to find. She used a fist to push the door open. In the entryway, the smell of blood and feces was stronger. She gave herself a little more visual acuity, and spied a leg protruding from the kitchen into the hallway. Silently she swore.

Not needing them, Claire left the lights off. The former Mrs. Rummell had been stabbed so many times that Claire fixed the number at more than twenty. The weapon, a butcher knife used to slice roasts, lay on the linoleum next to the body. Her senses already heightened, she listened to the house as she slowly walked around. Whoever had killed the woman was not within.

Heart heavy, she returned to the Journey, and climbed inside. She did not have to speak.

"Uh-oh," said Mollie.

"Yeah."

Paul woke up, and stretched and yawned. "Are we

there?"

A tear fled down Claire's cheek, and another. "It's easier being a werewolf than a human," she said, despondent. She twisted in the front seat. "Paul, I'm sorry. Your mother is—"

"No!" the boy screamed. He tried to get out of the car, but Claire locked the door. "Mom! Let me go! I have to see her!"

"Paul," Claire said gently. She did not know what else to say. What was there to say to him?

"You're sure?" asked Mollie.

Claire merely looked at her.

"Right. Dumb question." She reached for Paul, who was sobbing. He struggled against her, and inadvertently kicked her in the shin. She threw her arms around him and held him as tightly as she could, her lips moving against his ear, and making little soothing sounds. He continued to struggle, but his efforts gradually weakened.

Claire got out her Palmetto and called the police. She had to answer a full litany of questions, of which many of the answers she was ignorant. Informed that the police and an ambulance were enroute, she thanked the dispatcher and closed out, interrupting yet another question.

Sirens dopplered in, and toned down as the vehicles arrived. Claire stood at the side of the Dodge Journey, her empty hands clearly visible, as two uniformed police officers approached. They eyed her warily, and stopped to crouch a little when Mollie stepped around the SUV and drew up at Claire's side. She, too, displayed empty hands. Both women leaned back against their vehicle and waited.

The two officers each had flashlights, and shone them into the women's faces. Mollie shut her eyes; Claire squinted.

The shorter of the two officers introduced himself as Timchek. Addressing Mollie, he asked, "You called it in?"

"That was me, officer," said Claire.

The taller of the two broke in. "You're Claire De Lune?" she asked, after identifying herself as Cosgrove. "May I see some ID?"

Claire did not move right away. "I have to pull it from my hip pocket," she said.

"Go ahead."

Claire slipped her wallet free and pried out her driver's license, which she passed to Cosgrove. Something about the positioning of the two put her on edge. It occurred to her that they were regarding her and Mollie, perhaps not as suspects, but as persons of interest, even though they had yet to see the body in the house.

"Arizona," said Cosgrove. "You're a long way from home."

Claire shrugged. "I should've made a left turn at Albuquerque."

Timchek stared hard at her. "You think that's funny?"

"I guess not."

For several seconds he continued to glare at her, before shifting his attention to Mollie. "Let's see your ID."

She produced it and he examined it. "Also Arizona," he said to Cosgrove. "Who's that in the car?"

"His name is Paul," Claire answered. "He's the son of the woman in the house."

"What's he doing in your car?"

"It's not my car, it's a rental," she told them. "He's there because we found him on the highway back in Oregon and couldn't just leave him there. He said he had to get to his mom. We were going this way, so we took him with us."

"Just Good Samaritans, eh? Maybe you arrived while he was asleep, and went inside."

"No," said Claire, responding to the suggestion behind the question. She realized it was the wrong answer.

"So how did you know there was a body inside?" asked Cosgrove, pouncing.

"The door was ajar. I thought I should check."

"So you *did* go inside."

"Well, yes. But I didn't kill her."

"So you say." She looked at Mollie. "What about you? Did you go inside?"

"No," answered Mollie.

"Are you sure?"

"Quite sure," she snapped.

"The person you should be questioning is the boy's father," Claire put in. "He knew Paul had run away, and knew he was going to his mother's. I think he got here first."

"Want to know what I think?" said Timchek. "I think you two lezbos killed her so you could have the boy to yourselves."

"Larry," Cosgrove sighed disgustedly. "Jeez."

Claire took a step forward. "I think that's just about enough abuse from you, officer." She turned to Cosgrove. "Do you have any serious questions for us? If not, we're leaving Paul with you, and then we're leaving. You have our addresses. You know how to get in touch. If necessary, we'll waive extradition." She turned back to the Journey. "Paul, you'll have to go with Officer Cosgrove. She'll see to you."

"You lezbos aren't going anywhere," Timchek snarled.

"Are we under arrest?" Claire asked pleasantly.

"No," answered Cosgrove.

"I'd sure hurry on that APB," recommended Claire.

Cosgrove hesitated fractionally. "Would you two mind waiting until we sort this out a little more?" she asked.

Claire smiled. "Not at all."

The officers eased away, Timchek reluctant, and entered the house. When they were out of earshot, Mollie asked, "What are you doing?"

Claire shrugged. "I'm getting Timchek to bring himself under control."

"You mean, like hypnosis?"

"Oh, nothing so formal. It's an application of body language, facial expressions, and serious eyes. He's starting to feel less challenged now. A little trick we werewolves know."

"You are full of surprises."

Claire simply grinned.

Another two police vehicles arrived, followed by an

ambulance. Paul, still in the back seat, with signs of distress on his face, watched developments with questions in his eyes. Claire did not know what to tell him, or how to soothe him. He seemed more afraid of her now, knowing that she might transform at will. Claire's shoulders tensed as yet another police vehicle arrived, this one with but one occupant, evidently the patrol supervisor.

"Claire?" worried Mollie.

"If it comes to it," she said softly, "there are too many of them for me to deal with. Two, I can handle. More than that is problematic."

"Do you think we're in trouble?"

"It depends on the time of death," answered Claire. "I saved the receipt from the drive-thru. It has the time and date of our order. It could establish our lack of involvement beyond question."

Mollie was dubious. "And your best guess?"

"If everyone is interested in the truth," she sighed, "I think we're okay."

"What does that mean?"

"It means the police need a perp. And we're readily available for the role. Which is why, when asked, I will show that receipt to Cosgrove, and keep it well away from Timchek. He seems the type who would destroy evidence in order to secure a conviction and, perhaps, a pay raise." She reached out to Mollie's shoulder. "You are my beloved and my companion," she said. "I will protect you, and protect us."

Mollie could only nod as Cosgrove emerged from the house. Her face looked wan and drawn as she approached Claire. "The M.E. estimates the time of death as between two and three hours ago," she told them. "So I have to ask you: can you account for your whereabouts during that time frame?"

Without a word, Claire unfolded the receipt and showed it to Cosgrove without letting the officer take it from her. "We were engaged in a very late and greasy dinner around that time," she told the officer.

"May I have that?"

"No," answered Claire. "But I will allow you to photograph it while I hold it. I'm sure if worse comes to worst, my lawyer would prefer to have this."

"Yes, of course. Hold it still."

After taking several shots on her Palmetto, Cosgrove added, "We want you to come down to the station to make statements."

"I'll want my lawyer present during that process, for both Mollie and myself. As to timing, the morning will have to do, say around ten. We're tired, and we've been in these clothes for a few dances now." She gave Cosgrove the name of a motel. "We'll stay there tonight. But someone needs to do something about Paul."

"I'm afraid that won't be good enough," said Cosgrove.

Claire made a desultory gesture. "Then there will be no statements," she said, and tokked her Palmetto. Moments later, a man's voice was audible.

"Do you know what time it is?"

"Sorry, Sandor," said Claire. "The police here in Twin Falls, Idaho, seem to like us for a rather bloody and brutal murder." To Cosgrove, she added, "Sandor Hegyes is our lawyer." She watched the name register in the officer's eyes: a bit of shock, and uncertainty.

"The truth shall set you free, Claire," said Hegyes.

"Only if everyone is interested in the concept," she shot back.

"Ah. Understood. I'll be at the station in...two hours."

"Thanks," said Claire, and rang off. To Cosgrove, she went on, "Nothing until he gets here, and maybe not even then. Now, our car or yours?"

Cosgrove sighed. "We'll escort you front and rear."

* * *

At the police station, Claire and Mollie were handcuffed, searched, and escorted into an interrogation room, where they were seated at a table, and left alone. Unconcerned, Claire pointed out to Mollie the hidden cameras and microphones in the corners of the wall.

"Come here often?" she asked Mollie.

"Only on Ladies' Night. You meet the nicest people." Sighing, she shifted uncomfortably with her hands bound behind her, and added, "I just hope Paul's all right."

"I hope they had enough sense to put out that APB."

Mollie frowned. "You don't think they did?"

Claire shrugged. "Timchek didn't strike me as very bright. There's hope for Cosgrove, though."

"Do you really think it was the boy's father?"

"In a situation like this, that's the usual suspect," answered Claire, after some thought. "The problem is us. If we weren't there, they'd already have that APB out for him. But we're tailor-made suspects, because we were there, and because I told the truth, that I had gone inside. So we're the simple answer. Cops hate complicated cases."

"So why did you go inside the house?"

Claire smiled tolerantly, as if the answer should have been obvious. "Because I had to know," she said. "We certainly didn't want little Paul to go walking in on...that. And it's going to be bad enough for him as it is. His mother murdered, his father in jail, probably for life."

"If."

"Yeah, if. But that's why we have Sandor Hegyes."

"Is he...you know?"

"Yeah. And he does a lot of *pro bono* work in...that regard, for those who can't afford it." She cocked an ear. "Someone's coming."

Cosgrove and Timchek entered the interrogation room, but remained standing. He was a little too close to Mollie for comfort, and Claire wondered whether he had sensed that she was the weaker of the two.

"What time did you get to the house?" asked Timchek, his voice harsher than before.

"Me, or her?" asked Mollie.

Timchek swatted her across the top of the head. "Larry," said Cosgrove.

"I think he means me," said Claire. "You'll have to check your radio logs for the answer to that. I didn't look at the clock, but I called it in about ten minutes after we arrived."

"So you say."

"So I say," said Claire.

"I guess I don't understand why you went into the house," said Cosgrove.

"The front door was ajar—"

"So you say," Timchek broke in.

Claire sighed audibly. "You know, we don't have to answer any questions. But we're trying to help. If you keep interrupting our answers, we'll just stop talking. So choose. But choose wisely."

"Fuck you lezbo bitches."

Claire turned to Cosgrove. "Are you willing to testify against a fellow officer?"

Cosgrove blinked. "What?"

"I'm going to have our lawyer file assault charges against him, for striking Mollie. So I ask again, are you willing to—"

"*We'll* ask the questions," yelled Timchek. "And you *will* answer them."

"No," said Claire.

Timchek took a step toward her, and Claire heaved a deep shrug. Behind her, the metal chain that bound the two cuffs sprung, spewing fragments that clinked on the linoleum floor. Timchek yanked out his Glock and aimed it at her.

"Put it away, Larry," said Cosgrove.

"*Did you see what she—*"

Cosgrove had her own sidearm out. "Or I will shoot you, Larry."

Reluctantly he put the weapon away. "You turned on a fellow officer," he snarled. "You know what that means."

"Now get out of here."

He shook his head. "She's not handcuffed. She's dangerous."

"I'm terribly sorry," said Claire. "If you give me another pair, I promise to be more careful with it."

"Officer Timchek, I do mean now," Cosgrove said firmly. The firearm in her two-handed aim did not waver in the slightest.

"Don't shoot him," said Claire, her voice soft and urgent. "It's more trouble for you if you do. He's not worth it."

Timchek shoved his pistol back into its clip, and threw up his hands in disgust. He slammed the door behind him. Cosgrove gave him a full minute before putting away her own weapon. Claire and Mollie waited patiently. Finally, just as Cosgrove began to edge toward the door, someone knocked on it and opened it.

The desk sergeant took a step inside, and beckoned to Cosgrove, who departed with him.

"What?" said Mollie, frowning.

Claire shook her head. "Wait and see. In the meantime..." She got up and went to Mollie. A moment later, there was another tinkle of metal. Mollie got up, rubbing her liberated wrists.

"That's a neat trick," she said.

Claire shrugged. "Partial transformation," she whispered. "I can't do much more than that without exposing..."

Cosgrove returned, a look of distaste on her face. "I've been instructed to ask whether you intend to press charges against Officer Timcheck," she said, to Claire.

"Timchek should be gutted and broiled," spat Mollie.

Cosgrove suppressed a smile. "The boy's father was picked up about five minutes ago, on the Interstate. He had blood on his hands, arms, and clothing. You're free to go...although apparently you've found a way to free yourselves."

"Old equipment," explained Claire. "Buy American next time. As for Timchek, pressing charges will do no good unless there is corroborating testimony from a witness, and maybe not even then."

"Not this time," Cosgrove said grimly.

"I...see." She glanced at Mollie, who gave her a little nod. "You have our Palmetto codes," she went on. "If you need our testimony, just Palm us, and we'll come running."

"I will." Cosgrove swept an inviting arm toward the door. "The department will not issue an apology to you," she said. "But I'm sorry. I could have stepped in sooner. I should have."

"When you risk your job, it's not an easy call to make," Claire told her. "But you made the right one in the end. I'd like to know how it all turns out."

"As for the boy, Paul, Child Protectives Services will take him under their wing. At this point, there's not much else we can do…"

"Yeah," said Claire. "Would you please keep us apprised of his situation as well?"

"Of course I will."

Claire nodded. "Good night, then, what's left of it."

In the car, Mollie said, "Now what?"

In the east, daylight was winning its perpetual battle with the night. Already the sky was red and hazy, and only Mercury, low in the horizon, was bright enough to shine through. Without reply, Claire pulled out of the police lot and headed for the Interstate.

"Claire?" pressed Mollie.

Claire's lips tightened, bloodless. "She's a good cop. And she's going to be raked over the coals for this, if she pursues it." She tokked her Palmetto and laid it on the console. Sandor Hegyes answered immediately, and she brought him up to speed.

"The plane's about to leave," said Hegyes. "Are you sure?"

"Get on it," said Claire. "I want to retain you, yes, at your prices. I want you to represent a police officer named Jennifer Cosgrove." She briefed him on the circumstances. "And watch yourself," she finished. "Where there's one bad apple…"

"There could well be others. Understood. I won't do anything until after I've spoken with her, but I think the best defense here is to attack, starting with the local media. But that's my problem. I'll be in touch."

"So?" said Claire, to Mollie.

"Now what?"

"When we get back home, I'll set up a trust fund for Paul for his care and education."

Mollie turned to Claire as far as the seat belt would permit her. "Could we adopt him?" she asked quietly.

"It's hard enough in this country for two lesbians to adopt a child, male or female," Claire pointed out. "I can't even countenance how the court would regard a lesbian and a lesbian werewolf as parents."

Mollie laughed, and sobered. "Yeah, you're right. We'd lose our privacy. Paul wouldn't be a problem, but there are always those who 'check in' now and then to see how we're coming along."

They reached the Interstate and headed east toward the junction with Interstate 84. "Home-schooling, I suppose," said Claire. "That way he could travel with us."

Mollie was dubious. "What about sleeping arrangements on the road?"

"Yeah," sighed Claire. "That's all the religious freaks would need to hear about it." She mimicked a child's voice. "They slept together in the same bed, and do you know what they did?"

"We can get him a separate room."

In the same child's voice, Claire said, "They left me all alone all night."

"We could move to Sweden," Mollie suggested.

Claire responded with an exaggerated shiver.

"Okay, then, France."

Claire's hand jerked on the steering wheel, but she kept the Dodge Journey under control in the light early-morning traffic. "France? Why France?"

"I've never been to France."

"Oddly enough, that's a very good reason to go," said Claire. "Do you have a passport?"

Dismay lowered Mollie's shoulders. "No."

"No problem. I can get one for you in a couple days. We'll be in Salt Lake City in a few hours. We'll turn in the Dodge, and fly back to Tucson. Where in France did you have in mind?"

"South coast?"
Claire sighed. "*Mais oui.*"

004: Parlez-vous Awooo?

The airlines deposited Mollie and Claire at the Charles de Gaulle, one of the two airports that served Paris, and they passed through customs without a hitch. From there, they caught a local airlines to Grenoble, where Claire's International Driver's License aided her in renting a vehicle, this one a cherry-red, sporty Citroen C5 convertible. After gliding onto the E712, they headed for a town southeast of Grenoble.

"You've been here before?" asked Mollie, luxuriating in the comfortable bucket seat as Claire stayed with the early evening, rush hour, hundred-sixty-kilometer-an-hour traffic. The Citroen rode so smoothly that she was scarcely aware of the speed.

"Two years ago, I spent about three weeks in the general area," Claire replied. She glanced out the side window. "It hasn't changed much. But I did spend several days in the woods, and some time on the coast."

"I thought we were going to the coast."

"We will, we will. Tonight, though, we'll take a room, have a continental breakfast, and check out the *fromageries*."

"*Qu'est-ce que c'est, fromagerie?*" asked Mollie. "A cheese factory?"

"*Précisement, p'tite.* Part of the tour."

For no apparent reason, Claire slowed the vehicle. Behind her, cars honked and swerved around. She pulled over to the shoulder, slowed, and stopped.

In the dim light, Mollie's eyes widened with concern. "What is it?"

"One of us," Claire said quietly. "He's in pain. But I can't locate him...he's somewhere off to our right."

"In the woods."

"I think so."

She shook herself, then eased back into traffic without many objections. Taking the next exit, she swung the

Citroen through a quiet hamlet and headed back toward the woods on a narrow two-lane road that showed signs of recent repair. They came upon a roadside picnic area, with a single table and attached benches. Towering trees cast the area in darkness. Only the car's headlights enabled them to see it.

Claire parked on the dirt between two trees, and sat very still, eyes half-lidded. Mollie, who had seen her go into one of her sensitivity trances before, kept silent, even breathing without a sound. Her window was cracked open, just a little, enough for the chirps of nocturnal insects to creep in. Natural sounds would not disturb Claire. Now and then, a bird cried out, and there was the occasional hoot of an owl. But nothing else stirred within earshot.

Until.

The soft crunch of footsteps on dirt. Claire opened her eyes and glanced at the side mirror. Mollie adjusted the rear-view mirror so that she could see as well. A light and shadowy figure was approaching the Citroen. His movements suggested a confident diffidence, as if he were behaving quite naturally in uncertain circumstances. Claire rolled down her window as he reached the car's rear left fender.

"That's close enough," she called out, without looking at him.

In the mirror, Mollie saw the figure come to a halt, and wait there, poised.

"What do you want?" Claire asked.

The man's voice was young, almost adolescent. His French was clearly acquired in school. "I-I'd like...a ride, if..."

"Where to?"

"Any...anywhere."

"Claire?" worried Mollie.

"In the back," said Claire. "But we're not going all that far. We'll take a room in a motel in Romage. You'll have to find your way from there."

"Y-yes. All right."

"You're American?" asked Mollie, as Claire began driving back to the highway.

"English, actually," he said, his first words in that language. "I'm from Leeds."

Mollie did not recognize the city. "What were you doing out there?" she asked.

"Mollie," cautioned Claire. She then made introductions.

"I'm Gordon," he said, after a brief hesitation, and Claire knew this was a lie.

Flashing lights in the oncoming lane caused her to move into her right lane. An ambulance passed them on the way back toward Grenoble.

"Almost there," said Claire.

Gordon seemed perturbed. "So soon?" His sigh of resignation was audible. "All right, that's fair. Thank you."

"Where are you staying?" asked Claire.

"There's a youth hostel..."

She nodded. "I think I know the one. Look...you're welcome to stay with us for tonight. I mean, you'll get your own room, but I can let it for you."

"Claire?" said Mollie, twisting in the passenger seat to face her.

Claire waved her off. "Not now," she said tersely, and took the next exit.

Nothing more was said until Mollie unlocked the door to their room, at which point Claire handed Gordon his key card but invited him into their room. While Mollie, grousing incoherently, laid on coffee, Claire sat Gordon down at the writing desk with the motel stationery, and came to rest on the foot of the double bed, two paces away. As Mollie started to move to join her, Claire said, without looking at her, "Stay where you are."

For almost a minute Claire locked eyes with Gordon, who finally averted his by checking the closed door. Claire gave herself a little nod. "You're young," she said. "That's why."

"What are you talking about?" Mollie gasped. "He's at

least thirty."

"Thirty-two, in fact," said Gordon. "But hardly young."

"I was not referring to your human age," Claire said gently.

"Ah." He nodded to himself. "I was wondering."

"All right," said Mollie, exasperated now. "What's going on?"

"I smelled you right away," said Claire, to Gordon. "You'll learn to do that as well, if you can stay alive long enough."

"He's a," said Lyybie. "He's a..."

"Werewolf," whispered Claire. "And just turned. Two months ago? Three?"

Gordon nodded. "Two full moons ago."

"More than four years ago, for me," said Claire. "That ambulance...that was your doing, *n'est-ce pas*? You attacked someone. You have some control, but not during the full moon. Like tonight. It's not discussed, except among 'us,' but there are hunters, and you can bet they'll find out about your doings tonight."

"*Oui, je sais*," he said, and dragged stiff fingers through his shaggy black hair. "I know." He looked at Mollie. "Are you a...?"

She smiled with exaggerated sweetness. "No, I'm not. But I'm in love with one."

"Oh?" Then he got it. "Oh!" But something about the connection he made reached into his inner self. As he stood up, his dark eyes began to change shape, and his fingernails extended.

"Stop that now," Claire yelled at him. She took a couple steps toward him, already in the process of transformation. "Control yourself," she said in her werewolf voice. "Or I will control you."

His own voice deepened, just a little. "She's a she."

"She's *my* she."

Mollie punctuated Claire's declaration by swatting him across the back of the head with the TV remote. It shattered, and two batteries skittered across the floor.

To Claire, she said, "This was not your best idea."

Both had reverted completely back to human form. Claire said, "I can help you with your control. But you are the one who has to make the choice to control yourself. If you are not discreet, the hunters will find you and silver you."

"I-I…"

Claire flashed a grin. "That's 'Aye, aye, Captain.'" She drew a long breath. "Gordon, this is how it is. I'm older, more experienced, and an alpha. You are but a pup. Do not challenge me."

He looked contrite. "I won't, I…won't."

"This may be the only chance you will have to learn how to survive and live among humans," Claire went on. "So: stay with us by my rules, or leave and take your chances. Choose wisely, but choose now."

Gordon licked his lips. "Your…your rules?"

Claire said soberly, "There is no margin for error. Your odds of survival decrease with each rampage. And they are quite unnecessary. There is no purpose in biting and killing a human. *You're* human; that makes it murder. You're not going to eat one, because that's cannibalism. The only reason to attack a human is that you are out of control. Watch me; look at my hands."

Claire's nails darkened and grew to an inch long. Gordon's eyes widened. After a moment, Claire retracted her nails.

Gordon remained skeptical. "That's easy for you," he said. "It's the full moon."

Claire shook her head. "Not quite. One more day. But it's irrelevant. With control, you can transform at any time, or even not at all. But when you do transform, you restrict your hunting to deer and such." For a moment she tilted her head, regarding him. "Gordon, the rage you feel when you think the moon transforms you is really your fear of what is happening to you. Once you accept this status, this gift, you'll lose your fear."

"Gift," he snorted.

"You have it inside you now," she replied, her stare transfixing him. "Only in death will you lose it. You may as well try to use what you now can do, if and when such an occasion should arise."

He shook his head. "How?" he grated.

"It depends on the circumstance. If someone needs help, and salvation lies in your extra strength..."

"I saw her tear the door off a crashed car to save a child," Mollie put in.

"You can see better at night," Claire went on. "For example, when you're driving. You simply transform your eyes, and only your eyes. You also enhance your reaction times." She sighed. "Gordon, there's no manual for this. You may never even come across a situation where a full transformation is warranted. But you must be prepared mentally and emotionally for such an event. You must gain control of yourself, or be killed by the hunters."

"Who...who exactly are these hunters?"

Claire sat down on the bed. "They are special werewolves whose sole purpose is prevent the general public from being able to prove our existence. This is becoming more difficult, due to technology. If someone should record a werewolf...the result could well be a panic of the sort that got tens of thousands of women murdered in medieval times because the masses believed them to be witches. Notwithstanding that quite a few of them actually were witches."

"There are witches?" he gasped.

"I was just going to say," said Mollie, looking at Claire.

"Much of what we think of as supernatural is real," Claire told them. "They can't change you into a toad, but they have other ways of affecting people and outcomes." She crossed her legs and clasped her hands around a knee. "But that's not the issue here. I'm waiting for a response, Gordon."

"It's...it's too much." He put his hands to his head. "I have to think." He fumbled with his key card, dropped it, and regained it. Getting to his feet, he said, "I'll...let you know in the morning."

"No," said Claire. "Now."

"I-I..." He held up the card. "I owe you for the room,

but I have no money with me."

Claire dismissed this. "I'm not concerned about the money, Gordon. Your answer, please."

"I...then, n-no." He stepped unevenly to the door. "Maybe after I think this through."

Claire did not respond. He seemed to be waiting to hear her voice. After a few seconds, he opened the door and stepped out into the night.

After the door closed, Claire swore.

"Is this bad?" asked Mollie. Claire just looked at her soberly. "Okay, it's bad. How bad is it?"

Claire's bloodless lips tightened. "He's a young werewolf out of control and it's close to a full moon. If he becomes violent, he could expose the existence of others."

Mollie considered. "If there's an Underground, there should be some sort of program to help new werewolves adjust."

"There is," said Claire. "It's unofficial, and it has no name, but there are people who can be contacted. But the problem with Gordon is that I don't think he realizes that he has a problem." She shrugged. "It's not that uncommon among us. But...see, there's no 'cure' for this. There's no way out. You make the adjustments, and learn control, or eventually you'll be silvered."

"Like vampires," said Mollie.

Claire gave a light laugh. "Except I don't think 'garlic' is a verb."

Mollie's pale eyebrows merged. "Are there vampires?"

Claire patted the bedcover beside her. "Come and sit down, my child." After Mollie made herself comfortable, Claire went on, "Most of the myths I know of have some root in reality. Werewolves are not myths, as you know. We keep ourselves in the mythic as much as possible because humans tend to reject, often violently, those who are different."

"So there are vampires."

"Yes. There are. But remember this: humans, werewolves, and vampires have one factor in common, which is: all three started out human. I told you, with the transformation, you keep your attitudes."

Mollie nodded. "I get it. You reject those who are different."

"Me, not so much. But others do, yes. I'm more at peace with myself, and even more so now that you and I are together."

Mollie kissed her shoulder. "I'm glad I could help. But...vampires?"

"Are very old. They go back at least five thousand years in literature, which means probably another five thousand in oral traditions."

Mollie's eyes widened. "I didn't know that."

"In *The Epic of Gilgamesh*, his father supposedly was a *lillu*, which is a Sumerian word for 'a demon of the vampire sort.' It's the earliest reference I know of to vampires. Gilgamesh himself was a real person, although it's an open question regarding his relationship to the actual events in the *Epic*. Which means his father, the *lillu*, was a real person. And keep in mind that while Gilgamesh and his father might have been at least partly if not entirely mythological, the word *lillu* nevertheless refers to vampires. The Sumerians thought they were real; there must have been a reason."

"And...werewolves?"

"They go back at least as far as the ancient Greeks," Claire replied. "But that's not saying much, because they're two millennia later than the Sumerians. Supposedly there was a king name Lycaon who—"

"Lycanthrope," said Mollie.

"Yes. He tried to trick Zeus, and got turned into a wolf for his trouble. However, as proof of the existence of werewolves, this example is rather tenuous. There's nothing in that literature that suggests shapeshifting back and forth. Lycaon was in theory permanently a wolf. No *were* about it."

"But werewolves are supposed to eat people," said Mollie.

Claire shook her head. "That rumor didn't gain currency until medieval times, when the church was trying to frighten people regarding the supernatural, as a means of controlling them. Werewolves have killed humans, yes, surely. Eaten them? Not that I know of."

"Supernatural. You mean, like witches?"

Claire regarded her placidly. "There will be a quiz."

"Multiple choice? Maybe some true and false?"

"I was thinking essay."

"Cruel and unusual."

Claire paused, sniffing and listening.

"What?" worried Mollie.

"He's gone. Gordon's gone." She swore again.

"So what do we do now?"

Claire looked at the travel bags on the bed. "I think we should leave," she said. "This could get ugly fast."

Carrying their bags, they made for the front door. Claire opened it to reveal two gruff-looking men standing just outside. Mollie yelped, and ducked back inside.

Claire said, to them, "You're standing in my way. You don't want to do that."

Neither man displayed any identification. The closer—and taller—one said, "We need to speak with you."

"Claire?" worried Mollie.

"I think we'd better let them in," said Claire, and opened the door wider.

The taller one was Bridel, the stockier one Pierre. Neither sat, although the bed was the only place they might have done. Mollie, still a bit fretful, had taken a seat near the pillows but was deferring to Claire, who perched on a corner at the foot of the bed and seemed totally relaxed.

Bridel scratched his thick russet beard before each sentence. Pierre seemed content to let him do all the talking.

"The young man in the adjacent room," said Bridel. "The one you arrived with. Where did he go?"

"I'm sure I have no idea," answered Claire. "He's not with us, in the sense you mean."

"Explain, if you would."

Claire considered. She owed Gordon nothing after his refusal of her help. If the hunters were already onto him, she were best advised to stay out of the way. Still, she temporized by disclosing what she considered to be the minimum necessary information.

"I detected him from the highway," she began, "as we were on our way into Romage. I knew he was a pup, and I suspected the sirens we were hearing somehow involved him. After I pulled off and parked, he approached, asking for a ride. We brought him here, and I gave him a room. We had some discussion about learning control. He was dubious, and left. That was fifteen minutes or more ago. I thought he went into his room; at least, that was the signal I got from him. We were going to leave—I'm sure you understand that we don't want to be involved—and... *voilà*, there you are."

Pierre was looking intently at Mollie. "You are not of us," he said at last.

Her voice shook, but she said, "I am involved."

Pierre then turned to Bridel, who scratched his beard and said, "She can stay. As for you, what is his name?"

"The name he gave us was Gordon."

"The way you say that..."

Claire grimaced. "It surely was not his real name."

"Are we in trouble?" blurted Mollie.

Bridel ignored her. "You may leave here when you are ready. Should you encounter this 'Gordon' again, you are not to divulge this encounter to him. You know how to reach us. As, of course, we do you."

Claire nodded soberly. "I believe there is hope for him, if he can be made to understand that there are rules."

"That is no longer your concern," said Pierre, "if it ever was."

"Wait five minutes," instructed Bridel. "Safer for you. Safer for us."

Claire nodded grimly, and waited for the door to close before issuing a long blow of relief.

"That went well," said Mollie, with artificial brightness.

"I'd still like to help him," said Claire. "But this is way out of my hands now."

"What will they do to him?"

Claire shook her head sadly. "It depends on how far this has gotten," she said. "They may determine he is still salvageable. Or they may not." She got up, and once again retrieved her travel bag. "Let's just push on to the south," she said. "We'll find cheese and wine places almost anywhere in France. We can pull over onto a lay-by after a while, we won't have to drive all night. But right now our biggest need is distance: we need to put some between us and this place."

"I couldn't agree more."

With a bit of trepidation Claire cracked the door, and saw no one lurking about. Quickly they exited the room and practically dove into the Citroen C5. But Claire was under control, and drove in almost a stately manner as they regained the E712 and headed south. Presently the lights dimmed, and there were only the stars above and the high-beams on the concrete. Following signs for Cannes, Claire drove easily.

"You've been here before," said Mollie.

"I did mention it, *p'tite*. Lean back and get some rest. I'll wake you when we come to a spot for coffee."

"I'm not sure I can sleep, after all this excitement." She gazed out the side window for a while. "Those trees look eerie," she mused. "Like there's something inside them, waiting to get out."

"This is an old land," Claire reminded her. "Myths and legends abound in these places."

"Are there any werewolves about?"

She shook her head. "Probably not. I'd sense them if there were."

"Unless they were blocking you."

"There's no reason for them to do that, *p'tite*. I'm neither an enemy nor competition."

"Still, it's spooky out there."

"We'll be coming up on a low plains and a river shortly," she said. "And a small agricultural village. One or two places should still be open."

Only one small café remained open, and that only for take-out. Claire returned to the Citroen with a pair of hard-paper mugs of coffee and a small clutch of croissants. They sat in the dim light of the café window and took their snack. Mollie felt pensive and restless, though she could not have said why. Perhaps it was the surrounding darkness, and her suspicion that it was replete with lurking creatures from the Old Ways. She would have been hard put to define what she meant by that. Comfortable with Claire, she nevertheless had her anxieties about the real supernatural world.

"There's nothing to be afraid of," Claire said softly, and passed her another flaky croissant. "It's just a natural reaction to Gordon and the intrusion of the two hunters. They're gone now. We won't see them again."

Mollie pointed. "I think the wind is picking up," she said. "Look at those trees."

"You're right. It might be a squall coming up from the Med." She started the car. "There's a lay-by about ten miles ahead. We can pull up there."

Traffic, already dwindling, had become almost non-existent. Still, the highway was dark, and required caution to negotiate the curves around the sides of the hills. Claire could feel the wind effect against the front tires, and held to a firm course. As they crested a hill, they could see down into the valley that eventually led to the Mediterranean coast, and for a while Claire was tempted to push on to their coastal destination.

Blocked by clouds, the stars failed to appear. Only in the very low horizon were there a few twinkles. A little shiver shook Claire. Mollie was right: this was a spooky area. It seemed as if anything might appear out of the dark on either side of the highway. The land was old; the last ice had melted twelve thousand years ago. Ensuing civilizations had known creatures from the dark. She wondered how many of them had had roots in reality.

Something dark scampered across the highway: a deer, perhaps a wolf. Claire sensed nothing *were*. But the event left no doubt that the forests were alive. What she had told Mollie about Gordon now applied to herself. The incident with him and the hunters had spooked her. She was on her guard now. Her mind said there was nothing to concern her; her heart failed to agree with that assessment.

An oncoming vehicle flashed its lights at her, and she dimmed hers in response. Her vision reduced, even with werewolf enhancement, she slowed the Citroen to the speed limit. Behind her the night was pitch-black; ahead, even more so. A sign indicated a lay-by two kilometers ahead, but it meant a stop in the forest. She cast a quick glance at Mollie, who was now asleep with her head resting against the door, and winced at seeing her uncomfortable. Reaching into the back, she pulled the folded jacket up and tried to nestle it between the door and Mollie's cheek. This only served to awaken Mollie.

"Are we there yet?" she asked, her voice smoky and dry.

"About halfway. I'm going to pull over in a minute or so. We'll sleep there."

Mollie looked out the window. "In the forest?"

"It's just a bunch of trees, *p'tite*."

Shivering, Mollie hugged herself.

Something swooped out of the night and collided with the windshield. Claire hit the brakes, swerved, and managed to right the vehicle just as Mollie screamed. Caught against the wiper was some small animal with a full complement of bared teeth. To remove it, Claire started the wipers, only to see the creature cling to one like the last floating straw. The little squeaking noises it made in protest could be heard inside the car.

"What *is* that?" gasped Mollie.

"It's..." She shut off the wipers and slowed the Citroen. "Oh, my."

"What?" Mollie's voice trembled as she recoiled in her seat. "What?"

Claire's voice faltered as she pulled onto the shoulder, and then onto the exit that led to the lay-by. The parking spaces were empty. An old oak sheltered one of the spaces, and she pulled into it and, after a brief consideration, shut off the engine.

"Claire, what...?"

Already Claire had transformed fully into a werewolf. "Keep the doors and windows shut," she instructed, and got out of the vehicle.

While Mollie watched in horror, Claire gently lifted the wiper and allowed the creature to free itself. It seemed dazed as it began to crawl along the hood. Claire's lips moved, although Mollie was unable to make out the words. The creature—it looked like a bat—seemed to slow, then stop, and then...began to enlarge. Presently it became an adult female with long and rich obsidian hair, attired in black body tights and with a black cape that looked crimson on the inside. It slid from the hood to stand before Claire, who did not give way.

And Mollie knew immediately what they had hit.

"*Vous êtes une loupe-garoux?*" said the vampire, illuminated by the headlights.

Claire smiled, and waved a little hello with her paw. But she did not transform back to human. "*Bon soir.* I'm sorry we hit you. Certainly I did not mean to do that."

"My control was off."

Claire tilted her head to one side. "You are young?"

"There are no manuals for me to study," said the vampire. "As there are none for your kind, I imagine." Tentatively she extended a hand. "*Je m'appelle Thérèse.*

After some hesitation she accepted it with a hairy paw. "Claire De Lune. Are you all right?"

"I am glad you shut off the wipers."

Claire laughed. "Yeah. I don't know what I was thinking there." Her face grew serious. "Look, this is a bit awkward, and I know you can fly, but...can we take you anywhere? It's the least we can do after ramming you with our car."

"The fault was mine." Thérèse glanced through the windshield at Mollie. "As for the offer, I think perhaps...

that might be ill-advised. She is your friend, *n'est-ce pas*?"

"And she is protected."

"Yes. Yes, of course she is. May you have good hunting."

"And you," said Claire, as Thérèse soared back up into the night.

Even after Claire re-entered the car, she did not transform. She sat very still, paws on the steering wheel, attired now in rags, although she scarcely seemed to notice this. For several seconds she panted, before recovering her normal respiration. After a brief examination of the remains of her clothing, she said, "I seem to be dressed for the Côte d'Azur."

Mollie was more focused. "A vampire? There really are vampires?"

"I told you this."

"My life has taken strange turns," she mused.

"Are you unhappy about that, *p'tite*?"

Her reply was fervent, almost religious. "I wouldn't change it for anything. Um...are we going to stay here all night?"

"Is there some reason we shouldn't?" Claire countered.

"Well...where there's one vampire..."

"We can push on. I'm wide awake, believe me. Go back to sleep. We should arrive at the coast just in time to watch the sun come up."

The morning sky over the Mediterranean was just beginning to lighten when Claire pulled the Citroen onto a small parking lot within easy walking distance of the beach. Several other vehicles, including two campers, were already in the area, a few of them occupied by sleepers also awaiting the dawn. Claire, still shabbily-clad, dug a blanket from the back seat and covered herself while she nodded off. Mollie continued to drone on, her respiration light and smooth. Claire, however, kept one werewolf ear attuned to her and to the possibility of her nightmare.

Presently, as they were parked facing southeast, they awoke, blinking back the sunlight. Still in the blanket, Claire got out, opened the trunk, dug out some clothes—jean cutoffs, and a crop top that would have made it illegal in Amish country for her to raise her hands—and returned to the front seat to squirm into them.

"Didn't you notice the sign?" asked Mollie, in the middle of a languid yawn.

She made a little gesture toward the beach. The sign read, "*Le nu integral est formellement interdit.*"

"Complete nudity is utterly prohibited," Claire translated. "But it refers to going into town. Here on the beach, you can get a nice, even tan, if you wish. I'm wearing clothes, because town is the only place we can get something to eat." She was about to say more, but Mollie's hand squeezed her arm for attention.

"Do you hear that?" she asked.

Claire shook her head.

"It's a faint—a very faint—call for help."

Claire keened her *were*-hearing, and frowned heavily. "You're right." She looked around—in the rearview mirror, at the parking lot, the beach, out in the water, and even as far as the small yacht a couple hundred meters off-shore. No one appeared to be in distress of any kind. Claire fumbled for words. "I hear it, but it's...it's..."

Abruptly she paused, head tilted to one side, listening intently now. "Oh, no," she said. "Don't tell me..."

"What?" worried Mollie.

Claire scrambled from the car and got down on the ground to peer under it. Moments later she rose, a WTF expression crossing her face, and pulled out the blanket she had slept in. All the while, Claire was grumbling to herself. All the while, Mollie was gaping at her as if she had lost her mind.

On the ground again, Claire inserted herself under the car. Mollie felt the vehicle rise a little, as Claire gave herself a little extra strength to create room to maneuver. When Mollie leaned over to peer out the open driver's side door, she saw the blanket disappear under the car.

Presently Claire reappeared, the blanket now in a bundle, and slipped back into the car. After passing the bundle to Mollie, she started the vehicle.

"Keep it wrapped," she instructed. "Under no circumstances allow sunlight to penetrate."

Mollie stared at the blanket in her arms. "What on Earth...?"

"It's our friend from last night," said Claire. "It's Thérèse."

The unit contained a single room with a half-closed hygiene alcove for showers and ablutions. It was not in the sense of a motel room; Mollie referred to it as a room in a travel lodge, for those who had come to the coast to spend most of their time on the beach. The office included a registration counter as well as a little shop for postcards and trinkets, and a small but cozy café where one might enjoy a beverage or a light meal. The name above the office entrance was *Chez Maman*.

While Mollie carried the bundled blanket as if it contained a newborn babe, and sat down on the bed to care for it, Claire went about sealing off the interior. After locking the door, she closed the curtains in the front window and augmented that coverage with the comforter from the bed. The small back window in the alcove gained a covering of two thick bath towels. This rendered the room almost completely dark; only the votive scented candle they had purchased when they registered yielded any light at all, and that only enough for them to see what they were doing.

With great tenderness, as if the contents truly were a naked babe, Mollie opened the blanket to reveal the tiny bat, scarcely larger than her big toe. Gently she picked it up and placed it beside her on the bed, then slid away to give it room to expand. Over the course of two minutes, Thérèse took form, still wearing the black tights and the cape, her garments and appearance none the worse for having spent the night underneath the Citroen. She sat with her hands folded on her lap, and looking relieved.

"Are you all right?" asked Claire.

"*Oui. Merci.* Thank you."

Claire's countenance hardened a little as she leaned back against the wall and folded her arms over her chest. "What," she demanded, "happened?"

"I-I'm really very sorry, I'm..."

"Thérèse," said Claire, even more firmly now. "It's done. You're here, we're here, you're safe from sunlight. But we would both like to know why you...well, why?"

Thérèse hung her head a little, addressing her knees. "I realized when I flew off that I was in a poor...hunting area, let us say. You did not depart immediately, and so I was able to gain a hold on your roof, thinking that you would drive off to where there were more...to where the hunting was better. This you did. I did not anticipate that you would park out in the open. I had to take shelter after you arrived at the beach, and the only possible shelter was...where you found me." Following a brief pause while Claire and Mollie digested this, she added, "By the way, there is a tiny hole in the muffler, which would annoy me if I actually breathed."

"Yeah, wonderful, I'll have it checked out," Claire said drily.

"I did not mean to cause you any trouble," said Thérèse.

Claire laughed without mirth. "Too late." Her lips puffed out with her sigh as she stood upright, and away from the wall. "All right, you're here, you're safe, and you can stay till dark."

"I...yes, of course. Thank you."

"You were about to say," pressed Claire.

"I...did not...feed."

"Oops," said Mollie.

"So you need blood," sighed Claire, exasperated now. "That's just great."

"How much blood?" Mollie asked her.

"The measure is...I don't..."

"Well, what is it?" snapped Claire. "Five quarts? A couple of pints? Would you like a straw?"

"Claire," Mollie said softly.

She relented. "Sorry. But this is…is…" Calming herself, she thought for a moment. "It might be possible to take some plasma from a paramedic vehicle, if we can find one."

Already Thérèse was shaking her head. "How to say this," she murmured. "Plasma, to one such as I, is to whole fresh blood as water is to fine champagne."

"How much do you need?" Mollie asked once more.

"In your measure, I-I think perhaps two or three ounces," Thérèse replied, uncertainly.

"About half a cup, then," said Claire.

"Take it from me," blurted Mollie.

Claire took a step closer, and half-screamed. "Mollie, no!"

Mollie did not budge an inch. "No, Claire. I love you dearly, but you are and have been the supernatural half of this relationship. It's you who have done most of what we have accomplished. Now it is my turn to participate. I'm in no way supernatural, but there are some small things I can do. This is one. Thérèse, I choose, freely, to give my blood in this cause. What must I do?" In anticipation, Mollie bared the side of her neck.

Claire surged forward and tried to insert herself between the two. "No, Mollie, don't," she moaned. "You don't want to be a vampire."

Gently but firmly, Thérèse held Claire away. "She will not be," she said. "I promise you this. That is not how this works."

Claire struggled to remain between them. "I-I don't understand…"

"When I feed, or if I should bring a human across," Thérèse said carefully, clearly, "I do so from the carotid artery. Surely you know this. But we are talking now about a small quantity of blood to get me through the day while I sleep, and unto evening. That, I can take from the wrist. There is no danger whatsoever that this will turn Mollie. It is as simple as when a nursing technician draws blood for lab work."

"You're just saying that," groused Claire.

Thérèse got up and went to the desk chair. Deftly she broke off one of the wooden legs, and handed it to Claire before reseating herself. "If I am lying," she said, "stake me. Kill me."

"Claire, no," said Mollie, still not moving. "Giving blood is for me to do. You know this."

Claire's face contorted in anguish. Moments later, she eased away, eyes still watchful, but forcing herself to accept the circumstances.

Mollie's tongue flecked nervously over her lips. "Will it...hurt?" she asked.

"My saliva contains a numbing agent, rather like novocaine," Thérèse replied. "You may feel a slight pinch; nothing more."

"And...afterwards?" said Claire. "It will heal?"

"Yes, of course. After ten minutes, there will not even be marks."

Claire hefted the chair leg. "Thérèse," she said ominously.

Mollie extended her hand. For a second or two, Claire was uncertain what she wanted. A little gesture by Mollie added emphasis. Across two meters, their eyes met. Ever so slowly, Claire passed the chair leg to Mollie, who laid it softly on the carpet.

Thérèse shifted so that she was kneeling between Mollie's thighs. With slow deliberation, as if performing a ritual, she put her lips to Mollie's forearm. If Mollie felt anything from the bite, it did not show on her face. Instead, her eyes glazed over, as if she were on the verge of sexual ecstasy.

There followed movements of Thérèse's lips as she drew blood into her mouth. Not a drop leaked away.

The transfer of nourishment completed, Thérèse slowly withdrew, leaving behind on Mollie's skin two puncture marks, each the size of an aspirin. She sat back on her legs to gaze up at Mollie with sapphire eyes. "I thank you for your gift," she whispered. "The memory of this shall never leave me."

Mollie, still shaken by pleasure, could but nod. Thérèse rose to sit beside her on the bed.

"Now what happens?" asked Claire. Her voice was a little deeper, as if somehow she as well had experienced some of the intensity.

"I would sleep now," said Thérèse, "until evening."

"No, I mean...should we watch over you? Or stay here to, I don't know, protect you?"

"That is most kind of you, but: no, it is not necessary." She laid back, stretched out on the bed, and lowered her eyelids, and began to sleep the sleep of the dead.

A nudge from Claire got Mollie's attention. They hung the Do Not Disturb sign on the outer doorknob, and headed for the café and some breakfast.

005: Death Wish

"How's your arm?" asked Claire, after the server departed.

Mollie displayed it. Two tiny red dots the size of pinpricks were all that remained of the feeding. "It doesn't even itch," she said. She peered across the booth table at Claire. "Are you upset with me?"

"Not at all." Hair swished as Claire shook her head. "You made me realize that I have been shepherding you too closely, and depriving you of the air you need to breathe."

"I hadn't thought of it that way." She buttered another croissant. Flakes scattered as she bit into it. "I'm in your milieu, and we love each other. It's only natural that, being stronger, you would place yourself to protect me."

"But," pressed Claire.

"No 'but.' Well, maybe a little one."

"Which is? And wipe your mouth, you've got butter all over it." She heaved a mock sigh. "I can't take you anywhere, can I?"

Mollie flipped a napkin at her. "I sensed no danger whatsoever from Thérèse. Yes, she is," here she looked around, and leaned a little closer, "she is what she is. But in that moment, with me, it did not signify. She was a person in distress. I could help. I wanted to help. And I did." Her face twisted a little. "Please don't tell me I did wrong."

"You did exactly right," said Claire. "My caution was right as well, but I wasn't seeing her through your eyes, but from my own fears."

"It's all been a ride, that's for sure," Mollie acknowledged. "*Je ne regrette rien.*"

"It's far from over, *p'tite.*"

"You speak as if from certainty."

"Someone—maybe Mark Twain—said that life is just one damn thing after another," said Claire. She looked at the coffee carafe, and decided on one more cup, offering Mollie a refill, which she declined. "That's what ours has been since I ate the tofu in the store. But life is also a flow, a continuum, and it takes charge of itself and of us. For example, we went to Oregon to deal with Travis, but that was not why Life had us go there."

"Wait, you're talking about...about what? Fate? Destiny? You're saying that what we do, whatever we do, is foreordained? So there is no free will?"

"*Au contraire*, my croissant-snarfing love. We are free to decide and to act *because* we do not and cannot know what has been written for us. Everything we do, even abrupt and impulsive changes of thought or behavior, is already factored into the line of existence itself, the continuity of past, present, and future. But we *don't know* it."

"So?" pushed Mollie.

"So the real reason Life had us go to Oregon was to be in a position to help little Paul. Look at it this way: Travis was going to overdose, no matter what we did. There was no way for us to make a difference in his life—not that we knew this at the time. But our timely presence—and yes, timing was absolutely vital—kept Paul from being incinerated by that car."

"Wait. We don't know the car exploded."

"And we don't know that it didn't. Instead, we acted as circumstances dictated. Paul is safe. Which reminds me, I need to check in with Sandor."

"So why are we here in France?" asked Mollie.

"We don't know. We may never know. And the best bit is, it doesn't matter; we're here."

"To help Thérèse?" Mollie suggested.

Claire shrugged. "Certainly we're doing that, and are in a position to do it. Don't think too deeply about these things, *p'tite*. We live our lives. Sometimes this helps others. Other times, maybe not so much."

"But we didn't set out to help others," she pointed out. "Things just...happened."

Claire nodded. "One damn thing after another." She

glanced at the wall and said, "That clock can't be right."

Mollie turned around. Her eyes widened. "Quarter till *two*?"

"We'd better go," said Claire, and picked up the check. "There's some sunlight I don't want to miss out on."

The beach was not crowded, but most people there were active. Some walked, some waded, some played volleyball, and some stood around drinking and talking. Most were, in the words of the sign, "*nu integral*," or completely naked. A blanket from the back of the Citroen gave Mollie and Claire something to put on the pale white sand, and they started to stretch out on it, clothing still in place, when a volleyball bounced off Claire's stomach.

A young man with very short light hair came to retrieve it. After doing so, he stopped to gaze down at Claire and Mollie. No apology came from him. The words he spoke were rude, although the tone was pleasant enough.

"If you two skanks aren't doing anything, we could use a couple more players at the volleyball net."

Eyes narrowed, Claire frowned hard. Mollie said, "You called us *what*?" and started to rise.

He took a step back. "Oh, you're Americans! All right! I'm so tired of all the foreigners here. They don't speak English. They expect you to speak French or whatever."

Claire sat up. "Skanks?"

"Yeah, yeah. It's nude, you know. Lots of jiggling."

Looking at him, Mollie made a face. "And flopping around, I'd say."

"Hey, you coming or not?"

Someone yelled something from the volleyball area, and he dashed off.

"Saved his effing life," muttered Claire.

"Are we going to play?" Mollie wanted to know.

"I'm going to soak up a few rays and work on the contrast with my tan lines. You go ahead, if you want."

Mollie shook her head. "Not without you."

Sounds of the beach continued to fill their ears—cries of laughter, and splashing, and of someone suddenly getting wet. Claire tuned them out, and Mollie even managed to doze off, albeit fitfully. But the relaxation could not endure, and a moment or an hour or more later the sun was a sparkling reflection coming in low over the waters. The volleyball came by again, as did the young man with the Marine buzz cut.

This time he kicked a little sand at them. "Hey, we can still use a couple more players," he said. "C'mon!"

Claire rolled over and pushed herself up. "Might as well," she told Mollie. "We can use the exercise."

There followed a match in which little score was kept, and mattered even less. Each side had two men and four women. On one side, the play was serious yet fun, without—as far as Claire's French could determine—any remarks related to prurience. There were simply half a dozen people enjoying themselves and getting sandy. But on the other side...

The young man's name was Kurt. His favorite phrase seemed to be, "Set me up!" Regardless of where the players shifted after change of service, he always seemed to wind up on the front row, ready and eager to do damage. Whenever Mollie, who still retained some skills from high school, dug out an opposing spike and set up Claire, Kurt growled at her. The other man on their side, and the other two girls, both in their teens, tried their best to play properly and ignore Kurt, insofar as that was possible during play.

Finally, as the bottom arc of the sun reached the horizon, Claire and Mollie had had enough, and with waves and smiles at the others, walked away and headed toward their blanket, which had remained undisturbed while they were away.

"A bunch of naked women all over the beach," grumbled Claire, "and all a man has to do to look at them is look at them."

"They're all California girls," added Mollie, as they reached the blanket and began to don their clothes.

"I think a couple of girls cast their eyes on you."

Mollie tugged her jeans in place. "I'm spoken for.

They'll just have to take numbers and wait for my next reincarnation."

"Yeah. Where I was going with this, though, is here are all these women, and he has to look at you and me furtively. He'd rather peek than look, even though it's all there for anyone to see."

"Sick," said Mollie. "Sick, sick, sick."

"Yeah...oh, *poop*! Here he comes." Claire looked around, but there was no place to escape to.

"Hey, wait up," Kurt called out. He was still naked, but carrying a pair of black jeans and an orange muscle shirt. He was breathless when he reached them. "Hey, wanna go grab some beers?"

Claire did a casual eye-roll. Mollie said heavily, "Beer. In France."

A small cluster of Asian teenagers surged past them on the way to the waves. Kurt glared at them for a moment. "Damn Chinks," he muttered.

Claire stared at him. Mollie cleared her throat and said, carefully, "I think they're Japanese."

"Yeah, yeah, Jap, Chink, whatever." He hummed a bit, and sang an advertising jingle with words he adjusted. "You'll wonder where the yellow went when the H-bomb hits the Orient." He finished this by laughing at his own cleverness, adding, "Hey, I'll buy the beers, whadya say?"

With forced calm, Claire said, "I doubt you'll find Buds in the village." She bent, gathered up the blanket, and began to fold it with excessive neatness, totally focused on even corners.

"C'mon, we're the only Merkins in the place. Nobody else here speaks English."

"Oh, some of them speak English," said Mollie. "They just don't care to have it forced on them."

"Yeah, how would you skanks know?"

Claire's lips tightened to bloodless as she studied Kurt for a full minute, as if considering which piece of him to break first. In the harsh silence, his exuberance began to fade, and the hint of a question nudged his pale eyebrows together.

Claire looked at Mollie. Mollie looked at Claire.

"I've got an idea!" they said simultaneously. Claire deferred, but with a knowing look in her violet eyes. "I had the last one, Mollie. You go first."

She scuffed at the sand, as if hesitant to broach the reply. Finally she said, "We could take the beers back to our room, and maybe, you know, party a little there."

Kurt clapped his hands together. "Yeah, now we're talking!"

"I wonder if she's back yet," Mollie said, to Claire.

"She?" said Kurt. "There's another? Hot damn! Me and three girls. Party, party!"

"She said she'd be there by evening," Claire pointed out. She made a little gesture toward the sunset. "It's evening. She'll probably want something to drink as soon as we get there."

Mollie hid her grin by turning away. To Kurt, Claire said, "Just follow us."

"Oh, you betcha. You couldn't possibly lose me now."

"Then put your clothes on," Claire told him tersely. "You can't go into the village like that."

Kurt continued to warble on as they headed for the village. It was Mollie who finally got through to him. "Keep it down, Kurt," she said, her tone now severe. "It's a quiet party. Too much noise, and they'll throw us out."

"Yeah, yeah, I gotcha, I gotcha." He peered ahead. "Where is this place?"

"Almost there," said Claire.

She noted that the front window was still dark and covered. At the door she knocked first and called out, "We're back," before keying the door. Pushing it open, she found the candle still burning, and realized it was the second one she had bought—which meant that Thérèse was now awake. As they stepped inside, she peered into the shadows, and found the vampire standing at the foot of the bed, still dressed in tights and cape.

Upon spotting her, Kurt gasped. "Whoa, a Goth chick!" he cried out.

"Oh, yes," Mollie agreed. "She's very, *very* Gothic. Her

name is Thérèse. Thérèse, this is Kurt. He likes parties."

"Yeah," said Kurt. "That I do. Let's get it on!"

Claire held back. "Thérèse, I think Mollie and I are going into the village for some drinks. Meanwhile, why don't you and Kurt get, you know, better acquainted."

Kurt approached her, focused now. "Yeah, that's what I'm talking about."

"We'll be back in about...an hour?" said Claire, and caught Thérèse's tiny smile and nod.

"Don't forget to clean up," finished Mollie, and pulled the door shut as they departed.

In the café they took a booth by a window to watch passers-by and the night life while they drank coffee and puttered with some light pastry. Neither of them had much appetite at the moment, but they had no regrets, either.

"Do you think this is why we here, in this place at this time?" Mollie finally asked.

Claire chuckled lightly. "You mean the 'fate' thing? I really don't know, *p'tite*. There's no way for us to know, remember?" Her eyes narrowed a little. "Are you... having second thoughts?"

"Oh, no, not at all. Had that beach been empty, I-I don't know that he would have left it alive."

"You'd've had to get in line. I think at one point I might have been on the verge of clearing that beach."

"That would've made the ten-o'clock news."

"Yeah." Claire prodded her fork at the pastry, and finally pushed it aside. "Are you wondering whether we might have spared a part of the future?" she asked.

"Yeah, maybe."

"Perhaps we did; we'll never know. But if you're thinking of a tyrant or dictator, I shouldn't think so. He would have been more of a rabid follower, doing the dictator's dirty work. But...yeah, barring a Damascus moment, he would eventually have done some damage."

Mollie frowned. "Damascus moment?"

"Saint Paul began as a persecutor of the early

Christians," she explained. "On his way to Damascus, he 'saw the light,' quite literally, and from that point on was a changed man."

"Like when I realized that I was a—"

"I actually loathe labels. They are so limiting. Worse, they enable people who don't even like you to think they've got you figured out."

"Damascus," she said. "Paul. Got it."

"Are you about done there?"

They found Thérèse seated demurely at the edge of the bed, unblemished by her recent feeding. The room was in very mild disarray—Claire's night bag was on the floor near the desk, and one of the towels was missing from the bathroom window—but there was otherwise no sign of a struggle. They stepped inside and closed the door against the night, and waited to see what Thérèse intended now.

Pats on the blanket signaled for them to sit on either side of her. When she spoke, her face looked straight ahead and her voice included them both.

"Through this gift you have brought me this evening," she began, her accented contralto scarcely above a whisper, "you have shown me a path I wish to follow. It is in my nature to hunt and to kill. I do this two, sometimes three, nights a week. Until now this has been indiscriminate. But there are some—a few predators—who might well improve the lot of others by themselves becoming my prey. Such as he whom you brought me tonight. These are the ones I shall seek.

"But that is not why I wished to speak with you, Claire, Mollie." She turned to Mollie. "I did not tell you everything about the taking of your blood," she said. Seeing shock in Mollie's face, Thérèse hastened on. "No, it is no evil thing that I did to you, no. But the transfer of blood also creates a psychic link between us. We are now connected, Mollie. I do not know the range of this link, but I think perhaps it is continental. If you should ever need me, summon me, and I shall come to you."

"How...how do I do that?" asked Mollie.

"Close your eyes, think of me, and in your mind speak my name. I will always know where you are."

"I do not think you are as young a vampire as you pretend," said Claire. But she smiled as she said it.

"I was thirty-seven when I was brought across," Thérèse told her. "I am now, let me see, thirty-eight. But I am a quick study." She looked from one to the other, and added, "Especially when I am among those who accept me for who—and what—I am."

Thérèse turned a little to Mollie. Her hand went to Mollie's cheek, and brought her face within range. Softly their lips met, and clung in the candle light that cast them in shadows. When they parted, Mollie's upper lip stuck for a moment on Thérèse's before releasing. It was clear, even in little light, that the contact had shaken Mollie to her core.

The turn of Claire came next. The tenderness of the contact was the same, but as it lingered, Claire's nails grew a little, her ears changed shape and her tail rustled around in her cutoffs.

"You have a friend," said Thérèse, once again including both of them. Delicately she rose, and drifted to the door. It opened without her touch. The night moved in on them, and made the candle flicker. Again she looked from one to the other.

"*Au revoir*," she whispered to them, and was gone.

The candle went out.

006: The Odd Pod

The room remained dark to mid-morning; they had neglected to remove the comforter from the front window, so whenever one of them stirred, she assumed the day had yet to break, and went back to sleep. This continued until there was an awareness of bare skin, which induced a period of intense wakefulness, followed by showers and dressing.

"Options," said Mollie, over a continental breakfast of rolls, butter, various cheeses, and thin slices of different sausages. "Another and more peaceful day at the beach, or push on to...to where?"

"This trip was your suggestion," Claire reminded her. "What would you like to do?"

"After last night, I was thinking Transylvania."

Claire laughed. "I haven't been there, either. But it's summer, *p'tite*. That's seashore weather. Surf, tan, seafood, sand. We could drive the coastal highway to Cannes and Nice, where the pretty people play, and then move on to Italy or north into Switzerland and some different cheeses." She toyed with a few bits of *saucisson*. "It's not as if we're in a hurry."

"I think I miss Thérèse," Mollie said absently. "But she would be next to impossible to travel with."

"Yeah, that would be a problem. Sunlight is one of the luxuries you give up."

"I think by the time we finished with Cannes, I would be more interested in all those valleys in Switzerland."

"Good call. Let's take the rest of this to go, and go."

The relative lack of tourists and the absence of the annual film festival reduced Cannes to the status of a coastal city with crowded beaches. Although there were sights to see, including museums and some very old churches and other buildings, Mollie and Claire opted to press on to Nice, Milan, and then to Switzerland, but without haste, so that they might take in a sight or two along the way. This area of Europe was new to Claire as well as Mollie, and from time to time they paused here and there for a local meal, or a view of the older part of town, or even a tour of a Renaissance church.

Mollie was mildly astonished that Claire could enter a Catholic church, and suggested that she remain outside while she went into the Duomo di Milano to admire some of the stained glass. When Claire traipsed in alongside her, Mollie half-expected her to burst into flames.

Laughing, Claire said, "You're thinking of television vampires." Once inside, she looked around the dimly-lit nave, and after a moment or two she headed off to the right for a bank of candles that illuminated a statue of St. Francis of Assisi. There she lit a candle and slipped a Euro into the slotted bank that stood off to one side. In the quietude, the *clink* of it sounded unnaturally loud. Claire did not cross herself, but closed her eyes briefly. Moments later she turned back to Mollie, whose mouth still hung open.

"He is said to have loved animals," Claire explained. "I suppose if werewolves had a patron saint, he would be it."

"I-I don't know what to say."

Claire leaned closer, and spoke in a whisper. "I'm just like anyone else, *p'tite*."

"I still don't...don't understand..."

"Religion is symbolic," Claire replied. "Its meaning depends on the individual. For some, it means salvation. For others, and for me, it represents someone to watch over me while I make my way on this Earth."

"That might be the most religious statement I have ever heard," Mollie whispered back.

They slowly made their way up one side of the nave and down the other. A couple people in one of the front pews frowned at them when they crossed in front of the altar without genuflecting. Finally they completed the circuit, and stepped back outside into the sunlight, blinking.

A priest in black was standing at the top of the steps,

talking with an elderly woman. He smiled at Claire and Mollie as they passed. Uncertain how to react, Mollie averted her eyes, but Claire nodded and said, "*Padre*," adding, "*Che bella chiesa.*" His return smile acknowledged as much.

At the bottom of the steps, a costermonger was selling *spumoni*. Mollie bought two cups, with little plastic spoons. Walking around, they fought to consume the ice cream before the sun melted it completely. Street traffic was typical of Italian cities: frenetic and noisy. They had to scurry along the crosswalk to avoid drivers in a hurry. With the late afternoon rush due in half an hour, they finished their cups, got into the Citroen, and took the E35 *autostrada* toward Luzern, stopping for the night at the *Tureta* in Bellinzona, a small hotel north of Lugano, Switzerland.

The *Tureta* was a white, three-story cube with a row of arches across the front of the building. Under those arches stood a row of tables and chairs, where people might sit and enjoy a beverage or a snack and watch the Alpine town pass by. With no reservations, Claire and Mollie found themselves on the third floor, in a room with a window that gave onto the street below. Mollie drew the curtains—soft white with a few horizontal black stripes along the bottom—and sat down on the twin bed closest to the window, there to remove her loafers after the long day of travel.

"It's still early yet," said Claire, and checked the time on her Palmetto. "Well, maybe not that early. Nine twenty-two. But the café downstairs is still open."

"You've been driving all day," Mollie pointed out. "You need sleep." After a pause, she added, "And I'd like to drive tomorrow."

Claire acquiesced immediately. "We'll trade jobs, then. I'll navigate."

"Why Luzern?" she asked.

Claire flopped onto the other bed, slipped her hands behind her head, and faced the white ceiling and the chandelier. "Lucerne is just a waypoint," she replied, giving it the French pronunciation. "To the west is Emmental."

Mollie perked up. "Emmental? Like the cheese?"

"Only it won't say 'imported' on the label."

"Claire? These are twin beds."

"I noticed that right away."

"Did you want this one, by the window?" Mollie asked.

"Only if it is already occupied."

She put her loafers back on. "I think I could use a coffee and some pastry, after all."

The night was still warm, but only a few people were out and about on the street. They sat at the table nearest the café, which was attached to the hotel, and tried their Napoleon tortes, which were properly layered. Between them, silence reigned, and Mollie found this pleasant, and the moment reflective. The Alps around them—shadowed now by night—made her feel as if she were sitting in the bottom of a crater, with nothing to do save climb out of it. It was a fitting metaphor for her life so far.

The ascent had begun that night in the convenience store. Mollie thought back to it, smiling to herself at the memory. She had been cautious and frightened. She tried to think what she would do if such an encounter occurred now. She decided that she would like to think she would open her arms and say, "You want to dance? Let's dance." Not, however, that she would actually do so. Not unless it was Claire, seated now across the table from her...

She blinked, and brought Claire back into focus.

"You were far away," said Claire.

"Girl she wants," murmured Mollie.

"I've heard you say that before. Someday you'll have to tell me what it means."

"Tonight," she promised, and began to wolf down the rest of her torte. "After the love."

"So 'girl she wants' is your way of saying you try to live up to my expectations," said Claire, after their respiration rates had returned to normal and Mollie had explained herself.

"I hadn't quite thought of it that way, but yeah, I guess so," Mollie replied, after some consideration. "At least, at first. But I thought of it as my becoming the kind of girl you would want. 'Would' being the operative word. Later, as we went to Oregon, it morphed. The kind of girl you would want became the kind of girl I wanted to be." She made a face at the ceiling and the Universe beyond. "I'm getting there," she went on. "I'm becoming the kind of girl...woman...I want to be."

"I would say so."

Mollie beamed. "And here I am. Here we are..." She keened an ear. "I hear sirens."

"All cities and towns have them."

"Yeah. I was just thinking... You know, Gordon."

"How would he get here?" Claire countered. "More importantly, *why* would he come *here*?"

"Yeah," said Mollie. "There is that." She rolled on the bed to face her. "Wait, can't he sense you?"

Claire shook her head. "Not at this distance. That's only good for about a mile or so. No, this is probably a fire or a medical emergency."

"Or a traffic accident?" suggested Mollie.

"The Swiss are very good drivers."

"But we're in the Italian section of Switzerland," Mollie reminded her.

"Good point. Now go to sleep. We leave early tomor—"

Gasping, Mollie sat bolt upright. "I saw," she said, and pointed shakily at the window. "Something, I..."

"We're three floors up," said Claire, calmly. "And I didn't sense anything."

Mollie laid back down. "I was sure..." She sighed, and nestled herself in Claire's arms.

But it took her a while to get to sleep, and Claire's light snoring did not help any.

In the morning, after breakfast, Mollie drove. She missed one turn, but eventually wound up on the E35, bound for Luzern. The day was overcast and gray, and the highway was still wet with the rain from the storm that passed through. But relatively few vehicles shared the road with them, and gradually Mollie relaxed. In the sky north of them, darker clouds roiled—they were slowly catching up to the storm. From time to time Mollie's ears popped as the highway took them higher—one of the altitude signs read 1800 meters, or over 5500 feet. But the sign that got her attention read St. Gotthard Tunnel.

"We're going *through* the Alps?" she said.

"For about eleven miles," Claire told her. "Be sure to honk the horn halfway into it, so we catch the echoes coming and going."

"You're serious."

Claire shrugged. "What's a tunnel for, after all?"

"Eleven miles." Mollie checked the gas gauge. "Two-thirds of a tank."

"According to the map, there are some winding roads starting about ten miles before we reach the tunnel. If you want to lay up before going in, there's a town called Airolo where we could stop."

Mollie shook her head. "Let's push on. I want some of that Emmentaler cheese."

The Alps seemed to grow around them, like fangs emerging from a jawbone. Some were snow-capped and glistening, while others—mostly lower ones—had shed their white capes and were now basking in sunlight. Mollie's ears popped now and then as the highway took them up and down and back up again. Signs indicated St. Gotthard tunnel. They might have taken St. Gotthard pass around the mountains, but the long tunnel was irresistible. Inside the tunnel they passed two refreshment stops as well as an emergency station for gasoline, as it was a felony to run out of gas. But the eleven miles went quickly by, Mollie honked the horn at the halfway point and was pleased to discover that several other vehicles had the same idea. The cacophony echoed throughout the tunnel, until at last they emerged back into sunlight.

"Do you want to go back through?" Mollie asked.

Claire shook her head. "If we're bound for Luzern, we still have the Seelisberg tunnel ahead of us. But it's only six miles or so."

"It's still worth a honk."

"Stay on Highway 2."

The mountains seemed never to stop, nor did the changes in altitude. Presently, after the highway bent east for Luzern, they came upon the end of a great lake—the Vierwaldstätter See—and not long afterwards they entered the tunnel. Traffic was minimal, with scarcely a vehicle in the rearview mirror.

Suddenly Claire barked, "Stop!"

After a one-second check of the rearview for traffic, Mollie brought the Citroen to a halt on the narrow shoulder, and gaped in WTF wonder at Claire. Questions in her eyes died as they formed, for Claire threw open the back passenger door...and in spilled Thérèse.

Thérèse?! But Mollie had no time to ask.

"Go!" yelled Claire, as the vampire shut the door. To Thérèse, she added, "There're two blankets in the footwell. We'll be in sunlight in six more miles. You'd better get covered up."

"Thank you," breathed Thérèse, dragging the blankets into position. "Oh, thanks for stopping. I overestimated the time I had, and got trapped in the tunnel. Of course I saw your car approach. I don't know what I would've done if you hadn't come along."

"Probably you would have waited until dark," Claire said drily.

Thérèse laughed. "I was prepared to do just that, despite all the exhaust fumes. But then I sensed you two —the werewolf in you, Claire, and you, Mollie, for our blood connection—and I saw your car approaching."

"Are you all right?" asked Mollie, with a glance in the rearview mirror.

"I am now."

"We're headed for Luzern," she went on. "We should be there in half an hour or so. But it will still be daylight."

Thérèse considered briefly. "I can crawl into the boot until dark," she said at last. "If there's not enough space, I can change."

"What are you doing here?" Claire asked.

The vampire looked away, as if embarrassed. "I was on my way to southern Germany," she said. "For me, the hunting would be good there, with so many folk on the political far right."

Claire grimaced. "Not all of them are bad people," she pointed out.

"I shall be prudent. Now that I have my rule, it would make no sense for me to violate it."

"Did you feed last night?" asked Mollie.

"Well...no."

"Uh-oh," muttered Claire.

"If I leave tonight," said Thérèse, "I will be in Bavaria well before sunrise."

After a glance at Claire, who nodded reluctantly, Mollie said, "If you like." She did not have to explain further.

As the implied offer sank in, Thérèse said, "Perhaps from the other wrist this time."

"The tunnel ends ahead," warned Claire.

A moment later, Thérèse had transformed to a bat and crawled into the boot.

"Either you're going to build up an immunity," Claire said, a few moments later. "Or you're going to be brought across."

"If I'm going to be brought across," Mollie replied, in all seriousness, as the car emerged back into sunlight, "I choose to be a werewolf. But I think that as a human, I can be of help to both of you. We should form a triad."

"Seriously."

Mollie made a face. "Seriously, I don't really know." She paused briefly to reflect, and continued. "Claire, I'm a stranger in a new world. I love you, and I like Thérèse, though she and I haven't known each other long. She's had an impact on me."

"That's almost not funny," laughed Thérèse.

"And you do not regard me as a convenient blood

supply," Mollie threw over her shoulder.

"Watch the road," admonished Claire.

"Luzern, twenty-five kilometers," said Mollie. "Thérèse, you don't want to stay in the car until dark. We'll take a room, and bring you inside in a blanket. Can you eat regular food?"

"Slowly, and in small quantities, yes," she replied. "But it does me no good. I eat it only as a cosmetic activity. I think tonight, if you don't mind me leaving for an hour or so, I shall visit a blood bank."

Mollie glanced at Claire. "More pizza for you and me," she said.

For a few minutes Claire checked the road map. "There's a B&B on the lake," she said at last. "It's quiet, and the three of us can enjoy a nightwalk along the shore." She made a reservation on her Palmetto, and gave Mollie preliminary directions.

Once in Luzern, Mollie took a turn into the Altstadt, the older part of the city. There she found parking, and a *fromagerie* that excited both her and Claire. Leaving Thérèse to the secure darkness of the car's boot, the two went inside. Mollie found herself salivating with the first look through the display windows, even though the labels meant little or nothing to her. She found herself wishing that night had fallen so that Thérèse could come in and advise her. Claire seemed equally as lost.

Finally, taking a chance, Mollie asked for a small round of Tome de Provence and half a round of Chevrotin —both soft and spreadable cheeses—and three baguettes. She hoped the simple bread would honor the cheese. After several more minutes of looking around, they returned to the Citroen.

Having checked on Thérèse, Mollie once more followed Claire's directions, until they reached the B&B. It was situated up the slope from the lake, a dwelling with four bedrooms managed by an older couple whose children had left home, and serviced by a staff of four. It dated back to the 19th Century, but had been maintained and, in some cases such as the roof, remodeled. Check-in was uncomplicated, for their passports were in order, although Gretl, the clerk, looked curiously at the folded blanket that Claire was carrying.

There was no lift, only a circular staircase, which they negotiated up to the second floor. Number 2 awaited them just to the side of the staircase. The key Mollie had been given fit, but required a bit of strength to turn, doing so with a scrape of protest. The door opened to reveal in the light from the hallway a nicely-appointed bedroom with a double bed, a sofa, a stuffed chair, a writing desk with a chair in the desk well, and drapery over the single window thick enough to muffle sound. Claire flicked the light on, Mollie shut the door and secured it, and the two of them breathed sighs of relief.

Claire opened the blanket, and they watched Thérèse transform. Not an instantaneous event, it required some twenty seconds before the last feature, her nose, popped into place. Mollie and Claire exchanged hugs with her. To Mollie, it felt like a strengthening of the bond that had already formed among them.

"*Une triade, tu as dit,*" murmured Thérèse.

"And I'll have to learn French," Mollie sighed.

Claire chimed in. "We're more like a pod." She began to lay out the cheese and crackers they had bought for snacks. Thérèse looked askance at the display, but presently succumbed to a primal urge and tried a bit of the cheese. She chewed it thoughtfully and showed no sign of rejecting it.

"*Qu'est-ce que c'est,* 'pod'," she asked. "*Comme les petits pois? Comme une colle?*"

"Like peas?" said Claire, with a light laugh. "Not exactly." She proceeded to explain about dolphins and porpoises. At the end, she noticed Mollie looking out the window. "Something?" Claire asked her.

"Just some children playing in front of that house." She closed the curtains. "It's getting dark."

"And it is a full moon," added Thérèse, with a furtive glance at Claire.

"I change when I want to," Claire told her. "I have full

control over lunar impulses."

Thérèse hung her head. "I should not have said that."

Claire's fingertips touched the vampire's cheek. "Welcome to the pod, *mon amie*."

"Definitely have to learn French," Mollie muttered. "When are you going to visit that blood bank?" she asked Thérèse.

"Perhaps after they close." A bit of mirth radiated from her dark eyes. "Or is it that you wish to be alone with Claire?"

"Oh, that's something we haven't talked about," Claire put in. "Interrelationships." She sat down on the bed. "I'm sorry, Thérèse. You must be wondering where you fit in the pod." She patted the mattress. "Sit with me."

Thérèse did so, and Mollie took up the other side of Claire.

"If I say something in error, Thérèse," Claire went on, "please correct me gently, for I mean no offense."

"*Biensûr*."

"Am I correct in thinking that you enjoy from taking blood a pleasure that is sexual in nature?"

"Most times that is correct, *oui*."

"Ah, a French word I understand," said Mollie.

"So when you take blood from Mollie's wrist, what do you feel?"

Thérèse laughed. "I confess it is like foreplay."

"I believe Mollie is correct, not to want to be brought across—as werewolf or vampire. Our pod needs a normal human being."

Again the vampire laughed. "Understanding as I do now the nature of a pod, I say there is nothing normal about this one." A moment later, she added, "This may be why I am so...attracted to you. To being with you, *tout les deux*."

"Thérèse..."

She set fingertips on Claire's knee. "No, *mon amie*. I know where this is leading. For me to engage in full sexual ecstasy with either of you could well place you in danger, either of death or of the necessity of being brought across in order to continue living. *Alors*, medically I am dead, *je suis morte*. But you understand what I mean, *n'est-ce pas?*"

"Perhaps," Mollie said, "if you raided a blood bank or attended a Nazi meeting, you would be sated enough to be under control."

Thérèse shook her head sadly. "But no, *mon amie*, you do not understand. *C'est la passion*...it is the *passion* that I may be unable to control. In this, I cannot risk a mistake. As you say, we are a pod. I care for you, *tout les deux*. Both of you. So I may sample a wrist from time to time. That is all I shall risk. Insofar as it is within my powers—and they are considerable, as are those of the werewolf—I will neither harm you nor allow harm to come to you."

"I love you," said Claire and Mollie together.

"And I you two." She patted Claire's knee. "And now, I think I could sample a little more of that cheese."

007: Hunting Grounds

The snacks centered around chit-chat. Ridden with pancreatic cancer and given but six weeks to live, Thérèse had asked "a friend of a friend" to be brought across and, thereby, cured. In due course, this had come to pass, but with the usual cost to a vampire—no sunlight; a diet of blood, preferably human, and taken against the will; avoid beheading, fire, and sharp sticks. Some of this did not apply to Master Vampires such as Schenady, Thérèse's Master. Fire could be escaped by simple shapeshifting and flight. Sunlight could induce a powerful dormant state from which a Master Vampire might awaken at night. Sticks, if withdrawn quickly enough, left no debilitating effects. Decapitation, of course, was a problem.

"So Schenady came to you?" asked Claire. "What about afterwards? Are you his disciple? You said you had a blood bond with Mollie. Does he have one with you?"

"He does," answered Thérèse. "And I must obey if I am summoned. But he is a loner, preferring to hunt and to sleep. He has little use for an entourage." She flashed a grin, deliberately exposing extended canines. "I, however, have a pod."

"And if you took blood from my wrist," Claire went on. "What then?"

"If you wish the link to be between myself and the werewolf, you would have to transform before I take your blood," Thérèse replied. "I think. The legends are not clear on this, and as far as I know, which is not very far at all, such a bond has never been attempted."

"Probably because the werewolf would object," Mollie put in, chewing a chunk of smoked gouda. "But Claire is in control as a werewolf."

"There is also the possibility that if she were in werewolf form, the bond would include the human aspect as well." Thérèse regarded Claire with soft eyes. "Are you in fact considering such a relationship?"

Claire sighed. "I really don't know. But I'm curious."

"The gateway word to asking," said Thérèse. "In my case, I am glad I knew someone who could and did save me. I'm not sure the world is better off for it, though."

Mollie started to speak, but Thérèse raised her hand for silence while she keened her ears. "Someone's calling for help," she said, and got up from the bed.

"I don't hear anything," said Claire.

"Transform," Thérèse told her. Accompanied by Mollie, she headed for the window. The curtains pulled, they saw flickering light in a second-floor window of the house next door. Movement in other lit windows indicated the fire spreading. Flames licked at the entrance to the house. Out on the grass in front of the house stood several people, darting about as if they wanted to go back inside but were afraid of doing so, or wringing their hands in helplessness.

"We have to go help," said Thérèse.

Claire agreed, as did Mollie. The three of them dashed downstairs and out into the night. Reaching the nearest man, Claire spun him around to face her. "*Haben Sie die politzei getelefonieren?*" she asked, in poor German.

The man shook his head. A woman answered, in accented English. "They are five minutes away." She looked up at the windows. "There are children...a family..."

Mollie was horrified. "You left children in there?" She wanted to shake someone until pieces flew off.

"The fire is on both floors," said another woman. "We can't get through. The door is warped shut."

Partially transforming, Claire ran off for the front door. Behind her, people gasped. With the strength of the werewolf, she yanked it from its hinges. Mollie tried to enter with her, but Claire shoved her back outside. "You're human," she said. "Help those we rescue."

At the "we," Mollie turned back toward Thérèse. Already she was appraising the height of the second floor. "No!" cried Mollie, hurrying to her. "Fire, remember? You can't—"

"Have to," said Thérèse, and shot up with a vampire's speed to the window with the flames. With hardly any effort at all she tore the panes and frame free and cast the fragments down onto the grass.

Gasps of shock and wonder came from the adults on the grass. "Did you see that?" And, "How did she...?" And, scaring Mollie, "Must be a witch."

Somehow avoiding the flames, Thérèse dove into the room. Not two seconds later she emerged with a child in her arms. Again she flew, this time to Mollie. With the child released, Thérèse said, "One more," and flew back up.

By now, flames were licking at the front door. Distant sirens announced the approach of help. Mollie fretted. Fire was deadly to vampires; she doubted it did werewolves any good, either.

Suddenly a section of the first-floor front wall gave way, and Claire, partially transformed, stepped outside with a screaming child under each arm. When she reached a safe distance from the house, she released both children, who ran to a woman who reacted as if she were their mother.

"Thérèse?" gasped Claire, still half a werewolf.

Unable to speak, Mollie pointed up, where flames now licked at the shattered window.

"Oh, God," whispered Claire. "The fire..."

"Change back," Mollie advised her. "I think someone's going to the tool shed."

"It can't be helped. Are you all right?"

"I didn't do anything," Mollie said sourly.

"There was nothing you could do."

At another window, Thérèse threw a dresser through the glass, then flew out and down with the second child. More cries of fear and shock came from those waiting on the grass. Thérèse's clothes were smoking. She shed the light jacket and cast it aside.

"I am all right," she told Claire and Mollie. "Those people look...angry. Not angry. Terrified."

"They know what you two are," said Mollie.

Thérèse sighed. "*Alors*, we cannot have that."

The adults nudged the children behind them as she approached. Claire and Mollie trailed behind her. Before the throng stood Thérèse, arms at her side, her voice low and intent as she addressed them. Her words came slowly, evenly, like a meditative chant.

"The door was already ajar and the hinges burned free," she said. "I climbed up the drainpipe to get to the second floor. That is also how I came down with the child. With you two children," she added, to those whom she had rescued. "All of you were frightened and worried. What you saw was our help. We are happy that you are safe."

Monotome muttering followed from the throng. "Hinges burned. Climb drainpipe. Two children."

Thérèse turned away, breaking the hypnotic contact. The sirens grew louder, and flashing lights came into view. In a more normal tone Thérèse said, "We should stand back and let the firefighters and paramedics do their work." A little motion of her hand got Claire and Mollie to make with her a discreet exit.

When they were well out of earshot, Claire said to Thérèse, "Do you think it will work?"

The vampire shrugged. "For the adults, yes. The children are problematic, for they see things that adults do not see. But I doubt the adults will believe what they tell them."

"In any event," said Mollie, "we will be gone tomorrow morning."

"We should leave tonight," Thérèse said. "The sooner we are gone, the sooner we will be forgotten."

Claire nodded. "We can make Bavaria before dawn."

"As to that," said Thérèse, "I am not hungry."

They reached their house, clomped up the stairs, and packed. The discomfort of the owners at their leaving prematurely was assuaged by a hundred Swiss francs. In the Citroen, Mollie drove.

"We can make Baden-Württenberg," said Claire, her werewolf night vision enabling her to read the map from the glove box. "We can stay the day in a small town, and then..."

"*Alors*," said Thérèse. "*Nous devons parler.*"

Claire nodded. "Yes. We should talk. Here," she added, a fingertip to the map. "Waldshut-Tiengen. We can lodge at the Homestay; they offer private check-in and check-out. And the town is connected with major highways to the east. To Bavaria. Mollie, I'm a nocturnal creature. Pull over and let me drive. You get in the back with Thérèse and get some sleep."

"As you wish," said Mollie.

Dawn was half an hour from breaking by the time they reached Waldshut-Tiengen. Having memorized the map, Claire found the Homestay on a street where the buildings ran right up to the sidewalks, and parked in a nearby public garage. Check-in was routine, without so much as a frown at three women asking to stay in one room with a double bed. They signed up for three nights, with options for extension; Claire's credit card proved more than welcome, especially when she pulled it from a billfold that was stuffed with currency. A lift took them to the first floor—as the Europeans style it, to Mollie's confusion—and a room that overlooked the street.

With a worried glance at Thérèse, Mollie quickly closed the heavy curtains. In return, she received a smile of gratitude from the vampire. Claire sat down on the edge of the bed, her lips puffed out with her sigh.

"I'm exhausted," she said.

"You two take the bed," offered Mollie. "I'm the only diurnal here."

"All three of us can use some horizontal time," Claire told her, and patted the comforter beside her. "You used to work the night shift, so you're an honorary nocturnal, too. Besides, there's room for three."

"It'll be a bit intimate," Thérèse said.

Claire nodded solemnly. "I hope so."

* * *

The two nocturnals, true to their supernatural nature,

slept through the day, but after four hours of being sandwiched between them, Mollie decided to call it a night. Or a day, she laughed. The sound failed to rouse either of her companions, as did her movements to climb over Claire and get out of bed. Following a visit to the hygiene alcove, Mollie quietly garbed herself in a pastel green jumpsuit and black boots and went out for a bite to eat, laughing in the lift down that the notion of "a bite to eat" had different connotations for each of them. By the time she stepped out into the late morning sunlight, a different mood had swept over her. Idly she strolled past shops, detached from the products and the other passersby, until she came to a delicatessen.

There, in the display window, lay all manner of sausages and cheeses. Mollie recognized some of them, but the one that hit home was *blutwurst*. Blood sausage. Made from blood and, evidently, other meat by-products. Could Thérèse eat that instead of blood itself? Would she want to?

Quick shakes of Mollie's head and a shiver of her shoulders exposed the revulsion within her. No, Thérèse was...what she was. So was Claire. And this chain of thought led to the inevitable question: Who am I?

"The human comic relief," she muttered, without self-deprecation. Immediately she knew that was not fair. In the triad she had an important function, at least as far as Thérèse was concerned, for she could operate in daylight. As for Claire, the werewolf had long abandoned venison in favor of tofu. But what did Claire need?

Staring into her reflection in the display window, Mollie knew the answer to that as well. Claire as much had told her just after they had met: Claire wanted to be loved by someone who knew what she was.

Mollie now wondered whether Thérèse felt the same way. Or did that question emerge from the blood bond already between her and the vampire? She did not know, and she doubted she could inquire within the delicatessen.

She moved on. A clothing store, a tobacco kiosk, a

microbrewery. Here the smell of hops was rampant in the air. It was too early in the day for beer. Well, too early for most Americans; not so much for Bavarians. A glance inside at the bar spoke to Mollie of the popularity of the beverage at any time of day.

"You're not seriously thinking of that for breakfast," said Claire, behind her.

Mollie only heard the first three words before she let out a very short and high-pitched scream and stumbled into the display window. At the sound of the impact, patrons turned and stared from the counter inside.

"I've got you," Claire said softly, holding Mollie upright.

"I thought you were asleep."

"I was. Thérèse awoke me," Claire explained, keeping her voice down from the ears of passers-by. "It's that blood bond between you two. She sensed 'emotional distress,' so she told me. *Und hier bin ich.*" She pointed. "There's a coffee house with an outdoor patio. We can talk there."

They ordered simple black coffees that arrived in decorated ceramic cups and came with a small tray of rolls and cheese. A sense of uncertainty came over Mollie as she eyed Claire over the rim of her cup. Blood bonds were a part of the interrelationships, yet she had been taken from, and not been given. Was that true? Thérèse had taken from her, not to establish a bond but to slake a need that was later fulfilled with someone else. As for Claire and Thérèse…

"I have to ask," Mollie said abruptly, and set down her cup. "While I've been out, did you offer Thérèse…?"

A light smile toyed with the corners of Claire's mouth as she nodded.

"And?" pressed Mollie.

"We are bonded." Claire eyed her sharply. "Please don't tell me that distresses you. When she and I were talking about it earlier, you voiced no objection."

"Nor would I have, Claire. But I thought that in pod decisions might be shared."

Claire's countenance saddened. "Of course you're

right. I should have thought..."

Mollie looked away. "I feel left out..."

Claire took her hand. "I'm sorry. Oh, Mollie..."

She took her hand away. "I would have said yes. Or were you afraid that I would object?"

Claire did not respond.

"You never even thought about that, did you?" She shot to her feet, knocking over the chair, jostling the table and spilling some coffee. Without another word she strode away.

For a moment or two Claire debated whether to follow Mollie. Concluding that there were some things Mollie would have to work out for herself, she paid the check and returned to the hotel room, where Thérèse was still sleeping like the dead. A chuckle escaped Claire: well, Thérèse *was* dead. For a while she considered joining her on the bed, and instead opted for the chair at the desk, where she could gaze out the window.

The sun's shadows shortened to nothing, then began to grow again. Still Mollie had not returned to the room. Already Claire had begun to worry, and now she started to fret. She might search for her—the love bond between them enabled her to do that, to some degree. But the city itself weakened the connection. Had they been on a farm, she might easily locate Mollie.

Thérèse, on the other hand, might find Mollie easily, but for now she was unable to go outside. Still, Thérèse showed no restlessness as she slept, which told Claire that Mollie was okay, that her emotional state had lessened.

Or so she hoped.

Helpless, she slumped in the chair and closed her eyes.

As dusk fell, Thérèse suddenly awoke and sat up, taking a huge breath that she did not need. She slung her feet to the carpet and hissed, "Claire!"

Claire was already awake, and on her feet. "It's Mollie?"

"We have to hurry."

"Is it dark enough for you?"

"The sun is behind the buildings. That will have to do."

Though Thérèse could fly, they took the lift.

"Where is she?" asked Claire.

Thérèse's apprehension was palpable. "Alley. Nearby. I'm not sure."

After reaching the lobby, they dashed outside. Thérèse's blood bond with Mollie enabled her to know the general direction in which to find her. But Waldshut-Tiengen was replete with alleys and lanes. Many were used for deliveries to the stores and shops, and were cluttered with cast-away containers and boxes. Clair felt panic. Where, where? Few of the passageways were lit. People stopped and turned to stare as the two women dashed past, seeking, seeking.

And listening.

Abruptly Thérèse skidded to a stop by a filthy dark alley. She peered into the night with eyes only a vampire could see with. She tagged Claire on the arm, so hard that it knocked the werewolf back a step.

"Down here! Come on!"

They found Mollie at the closed end of the alley, on the other side of a dumpster. The lower half of her body lay in a puddle left by the previous night's rain. The arms were akimbo. The wallet was missing from her jumpsuit pocket. With nocturnal eyes, Thérèse performed a quick examination as she knelt beside Mollie.

"Knife wounds," she announced. "Side of the throat. Upper chest near the heart. Pulmonary artery punctured. She's bleeding out."

Claire looked around; no one was in the alley, or even paying attention to it. Unbidden, she transformed into a werewolf, but kept her Claire voice.

"What can we do?" she whimpered.

"C-Claire?" managed Mollie.

"Right here, baby. Right here."

"I'm...am I...?"

"Yes," said Thérèse, truthful but with forced detachment. "You're dying. I'm sorry."

Mollie's eyes fluttered to Claire. "Bring...across."

Thérèse shook her head. "That won't help," she said calmly. "There is only one way."

Mollie's breath grew more rapid and shallow with each passing second. "But...I...be dead."

"That is the price," said Thérèse. "There is no other way."

Mollie now managed a final strong breath. "I love you both. Both do me. Same time. Understand?"

"It might work," said Thérèse.

They bent down over her body. Thérèse at the throat, Claire at the shoulder. Thérèse scratched her own wrist, drawing blood, which she mixed with Mollie's. Even after Mollie passed out, they continued their ministrations, until at last Claire sat back on her haunches, and Thérèse reluctantly pulled away.

"Is she...?" said Claire, her voice taut with fear.

"Don't...don't know. Wait..."

"Thérèse...?"

"*Je ne comprends pas...elle vit.*"

"What does that mean?" gasped Claire. "She lives?"

"*C'est impossible. Elle est une vampire. Mais elle est aussi un loup-garou. Elle vit. Elle est une vampire vivant!*"

"She's alive? Are you sure?"

"*Écoute. Le battement de coeur.*"

Claire put her head to Mollie's chest. "You're right," she said breathlessly. "It's beating. Stronger and stronger. And look: she is healing."

"*Oui. C'est vrai.*"

"Oh, Mollie."

"*Elle est de nous, tout les deux.* She is of us both, *mon amie.*"

Mollie's eyelids fluttered, and lifted. With Thérèse's help, she sat up. At first she struggled to find her voice; when it came to her, it was strong. "Claire. Thérèse."

"How do you feel?" asked Claire.

"I don't know. I could stand a hamburger, fries, and

soda. After that, perhaps a visit to the next secret meeting of the Nazis in Bavaria."

Thérèse laughed.

"When is the next full moon?" asked Mollie.

Claire and Thérèse exchanged glances. "There is much you must first learn," said the werewolf, who was reverting as she spoke. "You have the powers of each of us, plus your own human aspect. We know nothing as yet of your vampiric limitations."

"Sunlight and sharp sticks," said Mollie, nodding. "But I feel no fear of daylight. A little of silver."

Claire grinned. "The pod is complete."

008: Destiny

Daylight had fallen for the three nocturnals. Already they had established that the sun had no effect on Mollie, except to assist her tan. Whole foods bothered her not a bit, but Thérèse discovered that she herself now had an improved tolerance for such foods, although sunlight still singed her. Now they sat in the hotel room, over coffee and rolls and butter and cheese, perhaps the oddest trio of supernaturals ever to have assembled under one roof.

"We could live in *der Schwarzwald*," said Thérèse. "We would be next to impossible to detect in one of those millennial oaks. Assuming we wish to remain in Europe, of course."

"We could base in the Black Forest," Mollie agreed. "But if we are going to do what I think we are going to do, we will need to travel anywhere."

"And what is it that you think we are going to do, *p'tite*?" asked Claire.

Mollie peered into her coffee mug as if seeking signs and portents. "We are vilified by almost all societies for our predations," she said slowly. "Because of our invulnerabilities, we hold ourselves to a different moral code. Humans say that we prey on them, and they're right, we do that. Some of us do that," she amended.

She swirled the remaining coffee in her mug. "What if our pod tries something different? Claire and I saved a boy from a crashed car. Claire and Thérèse, and to some small extent myself, rescued children from a burning house. Thérèse, although I'm sure lots of people would not approve, fed on a young man that society could do without—with the connivance of Claire and myself.

"The point is that, while it would be inadvisable to call attention to ourselves, there is some good we can do in the world. I propose that we go out and do that, wherever the tasks should take us."

They clinked their mugs together and drained them.

www.ingramcontent.com/pod-product-compliance
Lightning Source LLC
LaVergne TN
LVHW012023060526
838201LV00061B/4429